Something changed in her expression.

If he didn't know her as well as he did, he'd have missed it, but, even so, he couldn't interpret the emotion suddenly shadowing her eyes and fractionally tightening her lips.

When she reached out and trailed her fingers along his cheek, so lightly they could have been butterfly wings, he froze, startled by the surge of emotion engendered by her tender caress.

"Let me tell you a secret," she said, leaning in so her face was close enough that he could have kissed her, if he dared. "Sometimes it's far easier to accept your limitations than it is to fight against them and get your heart broken."

Before he realized her intention, Mina closed the gap between them and placed her lips on his. Soft and sweet and warm, they teased his mouth, moving ever so slightly, and now he recognized what he was feeling.

Desire.

Need.

But this was M

Mina!

Dear Reader,

Welcome to St. Eustace, home of the delectable Dr. Hezekiah "Kiah" Langdon. On finding his best friend, Dr. Mina Haraldson, depressed over the losses she's sustained, Kiah convinces her to travel back to the island with him.

There, she's surprised by the heat she discovers, and I don't mean the weather!

Mina was inspired by two family members who are amputees, particularly my granduncle, Dr. William Aird, who lost his arm in an accident. Family lore states that after the accident, he pulled over, used his tie as a tourniquet and then drove himself to the hospital. There, while the nurses cried, he cracked jokes to cheer them up.

By the time I was old enough to know Uncle Billy, it seemed normal to me that he had only one arm and was still practicing medicine. An amazing man, he didn't allow what could have been a career-ending event stop him.

My hope was to write a heroine with the same strength and resilience, even if, at first, she doubts herself and her abilities, and a hero to match her spark with fire of his own.

I hope you love Kiah and Mina as much as I do!

Regards,

Ann McIntosh

BEST FRIEND TO DOCTOR RIGHT

———

ANN McINTOSH

HARLEQUIN

MEDICAL
ROMANCE

Recycling programs
for this product may
not exist in your area.

ISBN-13: 978-1-335-14952-7

Best Friend to Doctor Right

Copyright © 2020 by Ann McIntosh

This edition published by arrangement with Harlequin Books S.A.

For questions and comments about the quality of this book, please contact us at CustomerService@Harlequin.com.

Harlequin Enterprises ULC
22 Adelaide St. West, 40th Floor
Toronto, Ontario M5H 4E3, Canada
www.Harlequin.com

Printed in U.S.A.

Ann McIntosh was born in the tropics, lived in the frozen north for a number of years and now resides in sunny central Florida with her husband. She's a proud mama to three grown children, loves tea, crafting, animals (except reptiles!), bacon and the ocean. She believes in the power of romance to heal, inspire and provide hope in our complex world.

Books by Ann McIntosh

Harlequin Medical Romance

A Summer in São Paulo
Awakened by Her Brooding Brazilian

The Nurse's Pregnancy Miracle
The Surgeon's One Night to Forever
Surgeon Prince, Cinderella Bride
The Nurse's Christmas Temptation

Visit the Author Profile page at Harlequin.com.

For my amazing and wonderful niece, Victoria,
and my granduncle, Dr. William "Billy" Aird,
both of whom have been inspirations to me.

**Praise for
Ann McIntosh**

"*The Surgeon's One Night to Forever* is a story about
meeting the stranger you never thought you will
meet again ever. Author Ann McIntosh brought
this story with emotions and medical drama.
A reader would stay glued to the book till the last
page to find what happens next."

—*Goodreads*

CHAPTER ONE

ALTHOUGH UNEXPECTED, THE sound of the buzzer heralding a visitor hardly registered.

Dr. Mina Haraldson lifted her head briefly off the couch cushion to stare blankly at the television, where a show she didn't recall putting on flickered in the gloom of her living room. Thick mental fog blanketed her more securely than the heavy quilt she was huddled beneath, giving her respite from the world. There was a vague recognition of something unusual having happened, but she had no idea of what it was until the buzzer went off again.

No need to answer, or even see who it was. She hadn't ordered food or anything else. Her parents, having been convinced their immediate presence was no longer necessary, had gone off to Florida for their usual winter break. Her brother was at home in BC. She knew that because she'd been forced to put on a happy tone the night before, for their weekly Friday night telephone conversation.

If she'd failed to convince Braden of her well-being, he'd have said something.

Somehow she must have done a good job. He'd

rung off without trying to interrogate her, taking her word that all was well.

Perhaps now that her medical career was over she should take up acting. After all, a one-handed actor was far more feasible than a one-handed surgeon. She'd put that on her "future prospects" list, if she ever got up enough energy to start one.

Tears clouded her vision, and she closed her eyes. Leaning her head back against the cushions and pulling the quilt back up under her chin, she drowned anew in her reality.

Her uselessness.

When the buzzer went a third time, her jaw clenched.

"Go away!"

The shouted words drowned out the TV and echoed in the apartment, but the person down in the lobby couldn't hear them, and the buzzer rang again.

Then her phone beeped, as well.

"Oh, for…"

Untangling her arm from the quilt, she fumbled around on the ground for her phone. Unlocking the screen, she squinted at the message, her heart turning over as she read it.

Answer the door, girl. Calypso Kiah is here and ready to party!

"Kiah?"

Shock dispelled the rage as swiftly as it had risen and was then overwhelmed by a rush of delight so intense Mina's head swam.

What was he doing here, now? He'd said he was going to Calgary for his cousin's wedding, then coming to Toronto to visit, but that wasn't until the twenty-fifth. Or was it the twenty-first?

Good grief, what date was it today anyway? What day?

She couldn't remember. Funny how, when you had nothing to do or to concentrate on, the days ran one into the other.

Obviously, she'd totally lost track of time.

Mina tried to sit up, was caught in the folds of the quilt and, in her eagerness to rise, put both hands down on the cushion beneath her and heaved.

Pain shot like jagged shards of glass up her arm from the nerve endings in her stump, making her fall, cursing, back onto the couch, dropping the phone as she went.

It was over a year since the accident, but she still forgot. Still tried to use her hand.

Still, somewhere deep inside, apparently hadn't accepted her left hand was gone.

And each reminder made her heart stop for an instant, denial washing through her, as strong as it had been the day she woke up in the hospital and learned about the amputation.

She couldn't find the phone, was still gasping from the pain, cradling her left arm against her chest with her right hand.

But it was Kiah, and she couldn't let him leave.

He was her oldest and very best friend in the world.

She hadn't seen him in person for five years.

Frantically kicking her feet, she freed herself from the quilt. Her cell phone was set up to unlock the downstairs door, but she'd never mastered the art of using it efficiently with one hand. So she tumbled off the couch and ran to the panel beside the front door to hit the intercom button.

"Kiah. Kiah, are you still there?"

There was a pause and, for a sickening moment, she thought he'd gone. Then his voice, deep and melodic, its island rhythm hardly distorted by the intercom, came through.

"Of course I'm still here, girl. You can't get rid of me so easy."

Knees weak, she leaned against the wall, a smile breaking over her face, silly tears once more filling her eyes.

"Thank goodness. Come on up."

As she buzzed him in, she was suddenly

aware of the state of her apartment. The unwashed cups, an old pizza box and wadded-up tissues littering the coffee table. The crumpled quilt, half on, half off the couch.

It was a mess, and she wasn't in any better shape, now that she thought about it.

When last had she even bathed, much less washed her hair? She'd been wearing the same shapeless sweatpants and sweatshirt for at least two days. For a brief instant shame racked her, but it wasn't strong enough to do more than mute her overwhelming joy and excitement.

After all, it was *Kiah*.

Pulling open her front door, she stepped halfway out into the corridor, her heart pounding as she stared down the hallway toward the elevators. Finding herself jigging from one foot to the other like an overexuberant child brought a bubble of laughter, but it stuck in her throat, burning, instead of breaking free. Emotions too numerous to recognize swamped her, rushing through her system in first hot and then cold waves.

When the ping of the elevator sounded from around the corner, Mina's world seemed to stop for an instant, and then resume in agonizing slow motion. It felt like a year before a shadow fell on the carpet; another eon passed before Kiah stepped around the corner and came toward her.

Bundled up to the hilt, as was only to be expected for someone who'd come from a tropical island into the Canadian winter, he was unzipping his parka as he walked. Through the haze of delight misting her eyes, Mina took note of the changes in him since the last time they'd been together. He looked older. New lines at the corners of his eyes, some gray salting the hair at his temples. But his smile as beautiful as ever: white teeth gleaming against his dark skin, the little dimple on his left cheek winking.

Just seeing him made something deep inside her shift, loosen, unravel. Where before she'd been lost in a fog, suddenly everything was in sharp, clear focus. Illuminated brighter than she'd expected. Dazzlingly so.

"Oh, Kiah!" she cried, as he got close enough to envelop her in a huge bear hug. "I've missed you so much!"

And, to her surprise and consternation, she burst into tears.

Kiah picked Mina up and carried her into the apartment, glad she had her face buried in his shoulder so she couldn't see the shock on his face, in his eyes.

This wasn't his Mina. More like a shadow of his friend.

The old Mina was always neatly put together, no matter the occasion. Even at the beach, or wearing jeans and a T-shirt, she gave off an air of tidy confidence. Not now, though. Wearing shapeless clothes, with stringy hair and a face sallower than it should be, even allowing for winter pallor, she'd been almost unrecognizable when he came around the corner. And when he hugged her, he realized she'd lost so much weight it felt as though she'd snap in two should his arms tighten too much.

Then there was the fact she was sobbing pitifully. In the more than twenty years since they'd met, he could count on one hand the number of times he'd seen her cry, and even on those occasions, it was nothing like this. She hated to cry, and always exerted Herculean effort to curtail the tears, indulging for a brief moment before getting herself back under control. Right now, she seemingly had lost every ounce of control she possessed, and it was kind of freaking him out.

Yet, growing up surrounded by women, Kiah knew what *not* to say to a sobbing female. So he sat down on the sofa and, pulling Mina's frail form close, repeated over and over, "I got you, sweet girl. Kiah's got you."

His heart ached to see her this way, but he was fiercely glad he was the one there with her, supporting and comforting, just as she'd been there for him all through the years, since the very beginning. Grade seven, to be exact. Mrs. Nowac's class.

He'd still been traumatized by and grieving over the loss of his father, terrified of this new school, the new life he'd found himself living. From the first moment he'd set foot in Moraine Academy, he'd known he didn't belong, and was sure he never would. The only way he and his little sister Karlene got into the prestigious private school was because his mother's employer, Mrs. Burton, had pulled strings and gotten them scholarships. And the only reason she'd done it was because it was the closest school to her mansion, and she wanted her housekeeper available in the mornings, not driving her kids to school.

They'd had to walk the four miles to school, since there were no buses going there. All the other kids got dropped off or, if they were old enough, drove themselves. As he and Karlene trudged onto the school property, he'd seen the scornful looks the other kids gave them, checking out their cheap, bargain-basement clothes and no-name shoes.

Karlene had noticed, too.

"I hate it here already," she'd said, loud enough to prove she didn't care who heard. Kiah hadn't replied. Normally he'd have tried to give it a positive spin, but just then he was overwhelmingly sad, really low on optimism, and couldn't in good faith disagree. He, too, was wishing he were back in their old school in Scarborough, surrounded by the friends they'd made the year before.

He'd walked Karlene to her class then made his way to the room he was assigned to, getting there just as the bell rang. Knowing the other kids would have seats picked out already, he waited by the door until the rest of the students had settled into their chairs, then looked up and found the last empty seat in the room.

On his way there he kept his head down, not making eye contact with anyone, yet aware of how everyone in the room was staring at him. The other kids' whispers surrounded him like the buzz of bees. Even all these years later he still remembered it, clear as day.

"We have a new student," Mrs. Nowac said, once he was seated. "Hezekiah Langdon. Please make him welcome."

"Hezekiah?" The derision in the boy's voice was accompanied by a kick to the back of Kiah's chair. "What kind of stupid name is that?"

The wave of laughter rippling through the class hardly mattered. Kiah already knew he had no business there. All he could do was wish things could go back to how they'd been—before his father died, and his mother had totally lost control. He'd thought coming to Canada would be exciting but it had all gone to hell. His father had been the one who held everything together and gave his children the love and support they needed, while keeping his wife's anger and bitterness in check.

Now that he was gone, the world was a bleak, frightening place.

If Kiah had had a magic wand, he'd have waved it and been back on St. Eustace. Probably running on the beach, or playing cricket with his friends.

"It's Biblical. Hezekiah was a king of Judea. You should know that, Justin. Isn't your grandpa a pastor?"

Kiah had been half-aware of the girl in front of him turning in her chair but thought she'd just been staring and giggling like all the others. When he heard her defending his name, he'd looked up and, for the first time, his gaze met Mina's.

She was so cute his heart stumbled over itself. Her hair swung around her fine-boned oval face like a curtain of amber, and her wide-set chocolate brown eyes, tilted slightly at the corners, twinkled. Later on, he learned she'd gotten her eye coloring and shape from her Korean mother, while the lighter hair had come from a trip to the beauty salon. Not that her hair was as dark as her mom's. Mr. Haraldson, her father, was almost white-blond, and in Kiah's estimation Mina was a perfect combination of her Korean and Scandinavian heritages.

"That's enough now, class." Mrs. Nowac had shushed them, causing Mina to turn back around and face front. Then the teacher started talking about the first lesson of the day.

"Smart-ass. I'll deal with you later, Mina Haraldson." Justin obviously didn't like being upstaged, and whispered the threat just loud enough for Mina to hear.

"Just try it," she replied, without turning around.

And despite his mother's firm injunction to keep his head down and not make any trouble, on pain of a thorough thrashing, Kiah turned and gave Justin a scowl.

"Yeah, *Justin.*" He made no effort to temper the swing and tempo of his accent the way he'd learned to do since moving to Canada, and the name rolled out like a dirty word. "Just try it."

When Mina glanced back at him and grinned, he'd suddenly felt better, as though life just might be worth living after all.

She hadn't had to befriend him. She was from a well-respected family and popular in school, not a misfit like he was, yet she'd gone out of her way to make him feel welcome and, after a little while, her friends had accepted him, too.

His mother hadn't been pleased about their friendship. Not that there was anything that made his mother happy.

"You have no business making time with that girl," she'd said, shaking her finger in his face. "You an' she no have nothing in common, and if she father find out 'bout you, he not goin' be happy."

"We're just friends," he'd protested, knowing how truly upset his mother was, from the way her English deteriorated into St. Eustace patois.

"Make sure you keep it that way," she'd said, turning back to the stove and rescuing the ripe plantains frying in the pan before they burned. "We don't need no trouble 'round here."

He knew what she meant, of course. The Haraldsons were rich, like Mrs. Burton, and he was a little black boy from nowhere—son of one of their neighbors' hired help. Kiah had believed his mother when she said Mr. Haraldson would be angry if he found out but, to his surprise, it had been the complete opposite.

Without Mina and her family, who'd treated him as though he were one of their own, he'd have been lost, and who knew where he'd have ended up? They'd been there for him during all the worst moments in his life, in a way his mother never had.

Witnessing his father's fatal heart attack,

barely a month before meeting Mina, had devastated him, left him floundering, unmoored. Mina's friendship had helped him get through it, just as it had helped him deal with his mother's increasingly violent rage. And when his sister had died, she was the first person he'd called.

She was the best friend he'd ever had, and now she needed him to repay all the care she'd given him.

As Mina's sobs abated, Kiah leaned forward, holding her with one arm, and snagged the box of tissues off the coffee table. Clearly, this wasn't the first crying jag she'd had, if the used tissues strewn around were any indication. Pulling out a couple, he thrust them into her hand, noticing for the first time how she'd crossed her left arm over her body and tucked her stump out of sight.

His heart broke all over again.

"I'm sorry," she mumbled, mopping at her face.

"For what?"

"For crying all over you, of course," she replied, burying her face back into his neck. "For being such a soggy mess."

He chuckled, as she no doubt meant him to, with the reference to one of the classifications they'd come up with for different types of people they'd met. "Soggy mess" was reserved for the whiny, weepy, complaining type. Not her at all.

And in his estimation, not what she should be apologizing to him for. She should be sorry for not telling him how deeply she'd sunk into depression, and for not asking for help. He was trying to formulate the right thing to say, but before he could figure it out, she sighed, and from the way she suddenly relaxed, he realized she was falling asleep. Then Mina conked right out, so abruptly he wondered how much rest she'd been getting.

Sliding down slightly in the couch, he made himself comfortable, cradling her across his lap. Eventually he'd transfer her to her bed, but not yet. If this was what she needed, he had no problem staying exactly where he was.

Reaching down, he gently took her left arm in his hand and lifted it. Mina didn't stir as her sleeve dropped down, revealing the site of her transradial amputation. He was surprised that she wasn't wearing a compression garment—a shrinker—since he'd read about the efficacy of its use for controlling edema, and how important it was for pre-prosthetic fitting.

There were so many questions he wanted to ask about how she was managing with the loss of her hand. Some of them he'd tried to ask her before, on the phone, and she'd brushed him off, wanting only to talk about her then-ongoing divorce from Warren the Worm. Just thinking about her ex-husband had his temper simmering, but Kiah pushed his antipathy aside. Now wasn't the time to indulge.

Just as it wasn't a good time for the dampness making him blink, as he looked at where Mina's small but eminently capable hand used to be. The last thing she'd want, or probably needed, was his sympathy.

She'd always been driven, in control, and fearless. Whatever needed to be done, she'd been there with a plan. Seeing her like this, drifting and seemingly broken, was almost too much to bear.

Lifting her arm a little higher, he pressed a gentle kiss just above the surgical site and then laid it back across her stomach, making sure not to jostle it. He pulled the sleeve back across to cover the stump.

"I got you, sweet girl," he whispered, before also kissing the top of her head. "Kiah's got you."

CHAPTER TWO

MINA DRIFTED UP from a dreamless sleep, the first she'd had in she couldn't tell how long. Despite her eyes being gritty, she actually felt rested. When had that become such an anomaly that she had to lie still in bed for a few minutes savoring it?

Then she remembered.

"Kiah!"

Dammit, she must have fallen asleep after crying all over him the evening before. Had he left?

Then she noticed the faint sounds of reggae music coming from her living room, and what could only be kitchen noises. And...

"Mmm," she muttered, tossing back the sheets. "Bacon."

When she opened her bedroom door, it was to indeed find him in front of the stove, his head and shoulders moving in time to the music, and she leaned on the doorjamb to watch him, a smile spreading across her face.

As though sensing her regard, he turned to look over his shoulder, and his answering grin warmed her better than any blanket ever could.

"So you're finally up, eh?" He did a little

shimmy to the music and waved the spatula at her. "Sleepyhead."

"Yeah," she replied, suddenly aware of her grungy state and bed head. "Do I have time for a shower before breakfast?"

"Sure," he said easily, turning back to the stove. "But don't take too long, or everything will get cold."

"I won't," she called, already heading back into her room, her stomach growling in protest of the wait. She could also smell ripe plantain frying, and it had been far too long since she'd had any of the island delicacy. He must have gone to the grocery while she was sleeping, since she knew there definitely hadn't been any food in the house.

Rushing through a shower, but taking the time to wash her hair, she tried not to think about the grilling Kiah was bound to give her after he fed her, if he even waited that long. They'd talked on the phone at least twice a month, often more, since the accident, and he'd tried so many times to find out what was happening with her arm. He'd couched the questions both as a friend and as a doctor, but there'd been a barrier inside her, a wall around everything to do with the loss of her hand, and she'd evaded answering.

It had been easier to tell him about how Warren had left her—although she was too embarrassed to repeat all the horrible things her ex had said. Like how she was no longer someone he was proud to be seen with. That her stump disgusted him, and she wouldn't be an asset to their relationship anymore. Only afterwards did she find out he'd actually been cheating on her from before the accident, and had planned to leave her anyway. The fact that he'd use the loss of her hand as an excuse just showed what a waste of skin he was.

So it had been better to talk to Kiah about her determined fight to ensure Warren didn't take advantage of the situation and con her out of more than his share.

Oh, and he'd tried. His underhanded double-dealing had completely opened her eyes to facets of his character she'd ignored all the years they were together. Warren had become, in her and Kiah's old parlance, a snake oil guy. It was totally in keeping with some of the things he had boasted of doing in his law practice, but like a fool, Mina had never thought he'd turn on her that way. Especially since he was the one who'd wanted to end the marriage.

Thankfully, his cruelty had spurred her out of the depression that had settled over her after she'd lost her hand, even if only temporarily. She'd hired a lawyer known in the Toronto legal circles as the Rottweiler, and the one female attorney Warren had admitted he hated going up against in family court. Jalissa Chang had made sure Mina got everything she was due, and a bit more, too.

Mina had been angry—mostly at herself—and that anger had sustained her. While she had known for a long time things weren't going well between her and Warren, she'd ignored the problems, putting them down to how busy they both were. In truth, now that everything had come out, and in light of the way he'd treated her, she wondered if she could ever trust her judgment of others again.

They'd been together since they were sixteen. How could she not have realized a long time ago how truly selfish and immoral he was? She'd also let him steer her away from motherhood by saying he wasn't ready, or didn't want a pregnancy to derail her career. He'd couched it in terms of delaying it, but now she saw it as a denial, and that was something she was having a hard time getting over. She's always wanted children, but at her age, single, unemployed, and with only one hand, that particular dream seemed unattainable.

As did most of the plans she'd once had.

During her darkest times, she'd known Warren was right to leave her, as useless as she'd become, but she couldn't condone his meanness.

So she'd concentrated on the divorce and everything that went into getting the separation agreement finalized. It had taken almost a full year, by which time she only had a month or so before the divorce, too, was done.

That was when everything truly fell apart.

She was always at her worst when she had nothing to do. Nothing to plan for or look forward to.

"Well," she said aloud as she rinsed her hair. "Now you have breakfast with your best friend to look forward to, so no feeling sorry for yourself today."

By the time she came out of the bedroom, all squeaky clean and dressed in something other than shapeless sweats, she felt better than she had in ages. Even noticing that Kiah had cleaned up the place brought only a small pang of guilt.

Something about being around this man always made her life better, and she was going to enjoy it for the short time he'd be in town.

"Come on, lazybones," he said, putting two plates laden with bacon, eggs, toast and plantain on the dining table. "I'm starving."

"I can't believe you'd call me that, Mr. I'll-Sleep-'til-Noon-If-I-Want-To."

"Ha," he said as he pulled out her chair. "Those days are long gone, now that I have Charm to take care of." The face he pulled was a mixture of fond amusement and a grimace. "I miss those days sometimes."

Glad of a conversational topic that didn't involve her arm or her divorce, Mina asked, "How is Charm doing? And Miss Pearl?"

"Charm is growing like a weed. It's hard to fathom that she's almost twelve already, and Granny is doing well, considering her age and the health problems she's had."

Kiah's grandmother had had a stroke just after he'd qualified as a general surgeon, and he'd been his niece's guardian for five years, ever since his sister Karlene's untimely and tragic death. Miss Pearl's ill health had initially drawn him back to St. Eustace, and although the stroke had been minor and Miss Pearl had fully recovered, he'd stayed. While Mina understood the appeal of home and family, she often silently lamented the fact he'd never come back to Canada.

She'd missed him so.

"Twelve, already?" Her mind boggled at the thought. Mina had been at the hospital when the little girl was born. It really didn't seem that long ago. "That's crazy."

Tucking into his food, Kiah just nodded, but she was all too aware of his gaze on her, at least until she picked up her fork and started to eat. Then he relaxed and concentrated on his plate, rather than her.

While they ate, he kept the conversation light, telling her some more about Charm—her dance lessons and determination to be a singer when she grew up—and his cousin's wedding in Calgary the weekend just gone.

"Was your mother there?"

Kiah shook his head and swallowed before answering. "I was worried that she'd turn up, even though she wasn't invited, but thank goodness she didn't. Apparently, I'm not the only person she's alienated and cut out of her life."

"No doubt," she agreed, knowing better than to ask if he'd be looking her up while he was in Toronto.

Kiah's relationship with his mother had been fraught for as long as Mina had known him, and he'd often said he thought she had an undiagnosed mental disease. Mina wasn't so sure. To her it seemed more like a personality problem. Mrs. Langdon could put on a nice face to outsiders, but to her children she was mean, selfish and controlling. The kind of person who, because they weren't happy, felt everyone else around her should be unhappy, as well.

Her assessment seemed to be confirmed when, after Karlene's death and Kiah's last big run-in with his mother, Miss Pearl had said, "I've known your mother since she was a child, and her parents spoiled her by making her feel she was the most important person in the world. Your father, God rest him, was such an easygoing man he continued that when they married. She never could stand it when she didn't get her own way, and has to take it out on everyone else when it happens."

That strained and often frightening relationship with his mother had scarred Kiah in so many ways.

Obviously not wanting to talk about his mother anymore, Kiah said, "I asked Roydon who in their right mind has their wedding in Calgary in January, and you know what he said?"

"What?" she asked, already chuckling. His cousin was a jokester.

"'Man, what better time to do it? I get to go off on my honeymoon to somewhere warm, while everyone else is here, freezing.' They're going to Mexico for two weeks."

"Hey, you can't fault his logic," she said, laughter making her lighter in a way she hadn't been in a long time. "Lucky them, heading for the sunny south."

Yet, even with the amusing conversation as he described the wedding and reception, she was on edge, knowing it was only a matter of time before he got on her case about her life.

He finished eating before she did, and leaned back in his chair, his coffee in hand. Mina immediately tensed. She knew that overly casual stance.

"I want to talk to you about something."

Here it comes.

Trying to be as nonchalant as he pretended to be, she made herself pick up a slice of bacon and wave it in his direction.

"What?"

Had she kept the defensiveness out of her voice? Mina wasn't one hundred percent sure.

"I want you to come to St. Eustace with me and register as an orthopedic specialist."

Dumbfounded, she stared at him, the strip of bacon suspended about two inches away from her lips, and like a ninny could only once more say, "What?"

Kiah must have heard the shock in her voice, because he held up his hand and leaned forward, all pretense of casualness gone.

"Hear me out," he said as she gaped at him. "There's a new Caribbean Clinicians' Union formed, and St. Eustace has joined. It gives new doctors a chance to go to various islands and learn from a variety of doctors and specialists. You can help us prepare, in the eventuality we're accepted into the program."

Mina just stared at him, still at sea, and Kiah made an impatient sound.

"Don't you see? We have great doctors, but this

is a whole new world to us. We're not a teaching hospital, so there is some confusion about how to put together a comprehensive training program. This is an area you're extremely knowledgeable in, and it's a great way to put some of that knowledge to use. And while you're there, you can upgrade some of our surgical abilities, too. It would only be for a month or two, or as long as it takes you to put the program together."

The pain that flashed through her was primal, the anger instinctual and blazing.

"Are you crazy?" Mina realized she was shouting but couldn't stop herself, and she got up so fast her chair toppled over behind her. "I can't expose myself like that, in a hospital. What use is a one-handed surgeon? Am I really even a doctor, still?"

She turned away so Kiah couldn't see how close she was to crying, and the rage left her as swiftly as it had arisen. Her shoulders slumped under the weight of the truth she was about to articulate out loud for the first time.

"Don't you see? I'm of no use anymore."

"Nah," came the stern reply, Kiah's voice hard, almost cold. "I don't see that. But what I do see is that you've become a coward."

Mia spun around so fast she almost lost her footing, and Kiah had to stop himself from jumping up to catch her if she fell. There was a sheen of tears in her eyes, but, as he suspected, she was once more furious, rather than sad.

He much preferred her that way.

"What did you say?"

She wasn't shouting now but speaking softly, slowly, and that was even more dangerous. But he was committed.

"You're a coward. Here you are, hiding away, letting all the knowledge you have in your head go to waste, and when I offer you a way back to life, you call me crazy. When you don't have a feasible argument, turn to insults, huh? Is that how things are going to be?"

Her jaw worked, as though she was trying to get words out, but they were stuck in her throat.

Probably choked by the rage he clearly saw in her eyes.

"What the hell is wrong with you, Kiah? Didn't you get the memo? I lost my hand. I can't operate anymore—"

"But you can teach and supervise, help us figure out how best to train the doctors that'll come to us," he blatantly interrupted her, which he knew she hated almost more than anything else. "Your skills have attracted everyone from sports stars to politicians to have you work on them. Why let that knowledge and experience, that reputation, go to waste? What else do you have going on? Oh, sitting around, crying and looking out onto the gray winter skies? Sounds lovely."

His sarcasm almost pushed her over the edge. She went so far as to take a step toward him, as though ready to physically lay into him.

"What the hell do you know about it?" she snarled. Literally snarled, with her lips curled back, teeth exposed. "How I choose to spend my time is my business, not yours."

Nodding, as though in agreement, would make her even angrier, so he did it.

"True, but when have I ever stayed out of your business? I'm offering you a chance to continue to do something with your medical career, and you're acting as though I'm asking you to single-handedly do spinal surgery on the Pope, with the Swiss Guard watching over your shoulder."

She froze. Went completely and utterly still, staring at him with an expression of something like bewilderment on her face.

"What did you just say?" she asked, almost whispering.

"I said, I'm offering you the chance—"

"No. No. After that."

He thought back, wondering what she was getting at, then slowly said, "You're acting like I'm asking you to single—"

Horrified with himself, he stopped. How

could he have been so thoughtless, so careless? There were a million other expressions he could have used. Why the hell had he picked that one?

Her lips twitched.

Tears filled her eyes.

Kiah got up, ready to apologize, once he got his voice back from wherever the heck it had gone.

Then Mina burst out laughing, the sound so unexpected, so sweet, it rocked him back on his heels.

"Oh, God," she howled. "Single-handedly..."

Relief washed through him like a heated wave, and Kiah couldn't help but laugh with her, even though his legs felt shaky.

Then they were in each other's arms, holding themselves up by the combined effort, laughing until Kiah got a stitch in his side.

Once they regained some kind of composure, he leaned back and looked at her.

"So I take it this is a yes?"

She wiped her eyes on her sleeve and snorted.

"Of course not." His stomach sank, until she gave him a grin and continued, "But I'll think about it."

And he knew, right then and there, that he had her.

So he grinned back and said, "All right, think all you want, but we leave next Thursday."

CHAPTER THREE

MINA WAS SURE Kiah's plan was one of the stupidest she'd heard in a long time, but despite her misgivings, less than a week later she was heading to the small Caribbean island of St. Eustace.

Every time she voiced an objection to the trip, Kiah had an answer.

"We need your help."

"No use wasting that expensive medical degree."

"You hate winter, anyway."

That one brought her up short, and she gave him a narrow-eyed glare.

"I do not hate winter. I taught you how to ski, remember?"

He'd snorted, a derisive sound he'd mastered by the age of thirteen and always knew just how to use to best effect.

"Actually, it was your dad who taught me how to ski. And I remember you grumbled the entire time about the cold. Après ski is more your style. Admit it, you're a bit of a disgrace to your Swedish heritage."

That led to a heated argument she knew she couldn't win but also couldn't resist engaging in.

Kiah had that effect on her, and she had to admit she loved it.

He'd also done something no one else had been able to do for over a month: he'd got her out of the apartment, and back into life. Between taking her out to eat and forcing her to go and get her hair done, Kiah wouldn't let her languish at home the way she wanted to.

Yet, through the laughter and teasing, the re-hashing of times past and the inevitable questions of "Whatever happened to...?" there remained a painful, raw spot in her chest. There was no way to avoid the awkward moments that arose, like when the salon owner asked if she wanted a manicure, or people stared when they realized she was an amputee. Grief welled inside her every time, reinforcing the little voice whispering, *You're no longer whole. You're deficient.*

The only person who didn't look at her differently was Kiah. Being around him somehow took her beyond the place of pain she was living in.

Now, looking out the window of the plane as it banked to come in for a landing, the sight of the verdant land ringed by aquamarine water along the beaches and rocks made her heart sing. She'd always loved the island and its people, and it felt amazing to have something to anticipate with joy rather than trepidation. After all, if she didn't feel up to the task of working at the hospital, she just wouldn't complete the paperwork Kiah told her the administration had prepared.

Despite his bullying her into the trip, filling out her paperwork was one thing Kiah couldn't do for her, and she considered it her ace in the hole. Her plan was just to stay a few weeks to catch her breath and, if she decided not to take up the offer of work, head back home. She still wasn't sure she'd be doing anyone any favors by pretending her amputation hadn't made a massive difference in her abilities.

When they landed and disembarked, she paused to take a deep breath of warm air, her spirits rising even more.

St. Eustace lay southwest of Grenada, just a little more than halfway to Trinidad, and was a little-known tropical paradise. Being back on the island, seeing the backdrop of lush, rolling hills in the distance, standing under the bluest sky imaginable, caused a bubble of happiness to rise into her chest.

Okay, so she had to admit the trip was a great idea. Not that she was inclined to share that information with Kiah.

But when she looked at him, caught him grinning at her, she realized he knew already.

Suddenly feeling like a two-year-old, she

stuck out her tongue at him, and his smile turned to laughter.

They would have gotten through customs and immigration a lot quicker if every other person hadn't stopped, wanting to greet Kiah, or Dr. K, as he was known. And every one of them gave Mina the once-over too, many outright asking who she was.

"This is my best friend, Mina," he told one elderly lady, slinging his arm over Mina's shoulder.

"Best friend? So when you getting married?"

Kiah laughed, and Mina smiled, too, but when he replied they really were just friends, the lady flapped her hands at them.

"If you find a best friend of the opposite sex, and you love them, you need to marry them. You think is so easy to find that?"

Then she stomped off, grumbling under her breath about the younger generation not having any sense.

Kiah and Mina chuckled together, and she couldn't help teasing him. "You've been saying that 'She's really just a friend' thing for more than twenty years. Aren't you tired of having to repeat it?"

Kiah squeezed her shoulders. "Ha ha. But yes. Sometimes. Especially when people give me that look, as though there's something wrong with me for having you as a friend."

He was navigating through the crowds as he spoke, steering Mina along with his hand, which was now on her back.

"I used to get that at university, too." She sent him a mischievous, sideways look. "But you must have realized that, since the other women on my dorm were always all over you when you came by."

Kiah pushed his lips out and twisted them to the side in impish derision. "I used to tell them I planned to steal you from Warren, just to get them off my back. Besides, at this point, I don't dare get married to anyone else. No woman would stand for me having not only a female for a best friend, but a beautiful one to boot."

Her heart clenched, and for an instant she was overcome with the ridiculous wish that he'd meant it, and they could go back in time so he could save her from marrying Warren.

But he was just joking, so she replied, "That's the most sexist thing I've heard you say in a long time. You should be ashamed of characterizing all women that way. Besides," she added, giving him another sidelong look, "that's just an excuse. You darn well know that's not the reason you don't have a girlfriend."

"Oh?" he said, letting her go to fish out the

car keys from his pocket. "So what's the real reason, Miss Smarty-Pants?"

"It's because any woman you're interested in would have to be intelligent, and if she is, she'd be too smart to be with you!"

"Damn," he said, staggering away from her, clutching his chest. "Straight through the heart."

And they were still laughing together as they got the luggage and then themselves into the car.

When they reached the house, Kiah's grandmother, Miss Pearl, greeted Mina like a long-lost child, hugging her so tight she squeezed the air out of Mina's lungs. Then she beckoned to the young girl standing in the doorway, and said, "Charmaine, come and say hello to Auntie Mina. You remember her, don't you?"

Charm came forward slowly, not out of shyness, Mina thought, but more cautiously than anything else. The resemblance to Karlene, her mother, was so strong Mina had to fight to keep smiling, suddenly wanting to cry instead.

"Yes," Charm said, her solemn expression not changing a mite. "I remember her."

"Well, give her a hug, then," Miss Pearl insisted.

Mina held up her hand. "You don't have to hug me if you don't want to. Why don't we shake hands instead?"

She saw Charm's gaze dart to her left sleeve and then back up to meet Mina's.

"Okay," she replied, holding out her hand to shake.

"Nice to see you again," Mina said, glad to note Charm had a nice, firm grip.

"You, too," the young girl mumbled, before turning away to grab one of the bags and head back inside.

Was she remembering that the last time she'd seen Mina was right after her parents' deaths? She'd been in shock, frightened and traumatized, but sometimes those were the memories that stuck with you. The aftermath of tragedy. The people who witnessed the worst days of your life.

"Hey," Kiah said. "Aren't you going to say hello to your favorite uncle?"

Charm paused and gave him a stare blander than dust. "You're my only uncle," she rebutted but stopped to give him a kiss and accept a hug as she went past.

They spent the afternoon settling in, and then it was time for dinner. Mina kept glancing at Charm, often finding the young girl looking back at her. But once their eyes met, Charm looked away.

She wasn't completely surprised when, as the

meal was winding down, Miss Pearl got down to brass tacks.

"So why aren't you wearing your prosthetic?"

Even though she'd been expecting the hard questions, she still balked when having them fired so head-on. But there was no escape. When she sent Kiah a pleading glance, it was to find him looking down at his plate.

Zero help there.

And she didn't want to tell Miss Pearl what she'd told Kiah: until there was a prosthetic available that could help her perform surgery, she wasn't interested.

So, trying to sound upbeat and matter-of-fact, she replied, "I don't have one yet. I'm still trying to figure out which one will be best for me."

That was when she found out where Charm got that drier-than-dust look from. Miss Pearl had it locked down.

"Humph," the older lady said. "You should have had one long ago. The longer you wait, the harder it will be to get used to it. And it's not as though you can't afford a really good, useful one, too."

"Granny," Kiah murmured. "Could you let Mina have a couple of days before you start lecturing her?"

"Humph," Miss Pearl replied again, as she got to her feet. "Charm, come help me clean up."

"I'll do it," Kiah said, pushing back from the table. "Your turn tomorrow, Charm and Mina."

And with a wink Mina's way, he gathered up the dishes and followed Miss Pearl to the kitchen.

Mina glanced over at Charm and found the young girl looking at her in return. This time Charm didn't turn away but tilted her chin up in the air.

"Why are you looking at me like that?" she asked, the defensiveness in her voice clear.

"Because I can't get over how much you remind me of your mom. I'm sorry I'm staring," Mina added, realizing how rude it must seem.

"In what way am I like her?" Charm shot back, looking as though she didn't really expect an answer that would suit, and Mina couldn't help chuckling.

"Well, not just how you look—and you do look a lot like her—but even just then, how you spoke reminded me of her. Do you know what her favorite saying was, when we were young?"

Charm shook her head, still looking skeptical.

"She'd always say, 'Prove it,' any time someone said something she didn't agree with or didn't know for a fact to be true." Mina felt a wave of sadness but tried not to let it show. "She didn't take any nonsense from anyone."

Charm considered that for a moment and then

asked, "Were you good friends with her? Like you are with Uncle Kiah?"

Mina shook her head. "Not as good friends. She was a little younger than us, and…" She hesitated for a moment, and then decided honesty would always be the best policy with Charm. "Well, your grandmother didn't approve of her hanging out with us. She'd let us take her to the movies or the fair sometimes, but mostly your mom had her own friends."

She was expecting Charm to ask why, but the youngster just gave a little frown and said, "Did you like her?"

"Your mom?"

Please don't be asking about your grand-mother.

Charm nodded, her gaze intent on Mina's face.

Heaving a silent sigh of relief, Mina nodded back. "I did. She was the kind of person who was honest with how she felt. You never had to guess what she thought. And she had a great sense of humor. One of those dry, slightly sarcastic ones, you know? But she was never mean. She didn't say things to hurt anyone, just told the truth, as she saw it."

A little smile touched the edges of Charm's lips. Then she glanced toward the kitchen before looking back at Mina once more, the smile fading.

"Granny Pearl and Uncle Kiah don't talk about her much."

Mina's heart ached, and it took everything she had to keep eye contact with Charm and not tear up.

"Sometimes, when something hurts so much, it's hard to talk about."

It was the best she could offer, but it seemed to satisfy Charm, who nodded slowly again.

Then, as if she'd had enough of that topic, she tipped her chin toward where Mina's left arm lay on her lap, and said, "So what happened to your hand?"

Taken aback, Mina didn't answer right away, and Charm frowned, her eyes narrowing. "Oh, I get it," she said. "You get to know every little thing about me, but I don't get to ask about you."

Mina couldn't help chuckling, although it came out of a throat that felt too tight for comfort.

"There you go again. You sounded just like your mom." Then, still being subjected to Charm's glare, she continued, "My hand got crushed in a boating accident."

Just saying it out loud again brought a rush of emotions—rage, pain and grief all wrapped up together. Charm's frown softened, although not totally going away.

"Couldn't the doctors do anything to fix it?"

Mina shook her head, the irony of it still bitter. "It was too badly damaged, and couldn't be saved. That's what I used to do, you know—fix broken, crushed and shattered bones. When I saw the X-rays of my hand, I knew even I couldn't have done anything other than what the surgeon who worked on me did."

There were footsteps in the hallway leading from the kitchen, and when Kiah came into the dining room, both Mina and Charm turned to look at him.

"What are you two up to in here?" he asked, giving them an exaggeratedly suspicious glance.

Totally deadpan, Charm responded, "Plotting to take over the world."

"Well," he shot back as Mina sputtered into laughter. "I'm sorry to interrupt the planning session, but it's time for you to start getting ready for bed. All your homework done?"

"Yes," Charm said. "I didn't have a lot. Just some math problems, and they were easy-peasy."

"Lemon-squeezy?" Kiah tacked on, making it a question.

"You know it," she replied, pushing back her chair and getting up. "Mrs. Hastings is talking about letting me do some advanced work for the rest of the year. I brought home a note about it but told her she'd have to wait for you to get back before she got an answer."

"I'll take a look at it tomorrow," Kiah said, snagging Charm as she was going by and pulling her in for a hug.

Even though Charm said, "Uncle," in a disgusted tone, Mina saw how she rested her head against Kiah's chest and smiled when he planted a kiss on the top of her head.

"Have your shower, and then you can read for half an hour before it's lights out, okay?"

"It's still early," Charm said, ducking out of the hug and heading for her room. "If I hurry up and bathe, can I read for an hour?"

"Bathe properly, and then forty-five minutes."

"Deal," came her answer from down the hall.

Kiah gazed after her for a moment, and then turned his smile on Mina. Something about the tender set of his lips melted her heart, and she smiled back.

"If I don't keep an eye on her, she'd stay up all night reading," he said, holding out his hand to Mina. "Let's go sit outside for a while. There's a nice breeze tonight."

Instinctively she took that outstretched hand, and then everything froze, just for an instant.

Something shifted inside as an indescribable sensation crashed through her, causing a jolt of adrenaline, sharpening her consciousness so that she saw Kiah as though for the first time. Became aware of his beauty anew, just as she had so long ago when she'd watched him walk past her desk on the first day he'd come to school.

And as though to emphasize the strangeness of it all, she caught a hint of his scent, warm and woodsy, as familiar to her as her own, and yet suddenly different, too. Not that it had changed, but it was somehow interpreted in a new way, so that her pulse began to pound and warmth flooded her belly.

"Mina?" Kiah's gaze sharpened, became probing. "You all right?"

The words shocked her out of whatever the heck she'd been going through, and she blinked, as though awaking from a dream.

"What? Yes, I'm fine," she replied, getting to her feet, firmly shaking off the last vestiges of her strange mental hiatus, although they wanted to cling, like cobwebs. "Just woolgathering for a second. Lead the way."

Kiah didn't move immediately, just held her hand, his fingers firm and strong around hers. "You sure?"

"Of course I'm sure. Come on. I could use a little cool breeze just about now."

And that was no word of a lie. In fact, she'd go so far as to say she could use a cold shower.

The lingering effects of whatever she'd just gone through felt suspiciously like arousal.

But that was impossible.

Wasn't it?

"You Canadians and your inability to enjoy whatever the weather is. You constantly complain about it being too hot, or too cold, or too wet, or whatever."

His teasing words were exactly what she needed and led to a spirited argument about his expecting her to not feel the heat when coming out of the winter's cold. But even while they were going back and forth with each other, she felt his gaze on her and knew something had irrevocably changed.

Now she needed to figure out what it was.

CHAPTER FOUR

SINCE HE WASN'T back on call until the Sunday night after their arrival on St. Eustace, Kiah's plan had been to take Mina around and reacquaint her with the island. That went out the window when, the day after they got there, he was called in for an emergency meeting at the hospital, in his capacity as a member of the medical board. In addition to being a surgeon, he wore many hats at the hospital, since the island was small and the number of doctors to call on wasn't large, either.

"There've been reports of possible cases of the chikungunya viral disease in Trinidad, and because we have a lot of people going back and forth between the islands, the minister of health wants to make sure our action plan is solid. Miss Pearl is going, too, since she's the head of the district nurse program, so you might as well come along with us. You can nose around the hospital while we're in the meeting. Maybe even sign the rest of the paperwork so they can finalize your work permit."

Mina was still sitting at the dining table, finishing the last of her coffee, and when she looked up, Kiah saw the refusal in her eyes without her saying a word. He had a battery of answers to combat her excuses, but before they got to that point, his grandmother came into the room.

Miss Pearl gave Mina a visual once-over and then said, "That's too casual for the hospital. Hurry up and change into something else, or we'll be late."

To his surprise, after a short pause, Mina got up.

"Okay," she replied, shocking Kiah with her meek acquiescence. "Give me a few minutes."

Kiah watched her retreating back for a moment, before turning and finding his grandmother's steely gaze resting on him.

Before she could say anything else, he forestalled her with an upraised hand. "And no, although I'm still nominally on vacation, I don't plan to wear these flip-flops to the hospital."

But Miss Pearl didn't seem interested in his casual footwear. Instead, she said, "We should include Mina in the meeting with the minister."

"Why, Granny? She's an orthopedic specialist, not an epidemiologist."

His grandmother gave him a scathing glare, then moved closer, lowering her voice to say, "Use your head, Hezekiah. How long do you think she'll be satisfied by writing manuals and formulating procedures? She's in transition, but eventually she's going to have to figure out what she wants to do next."

"And how will this benefit her?" he asked, trying not to let his irritation show in his tone. If anyone was going to help Mina, it should be him, not his grandmother.

Miss Pearl narrowed her eyes. "She has to be reminded she was a doctor first, before a surgeon. There are a lot of options open to her, but until she realizes that, she'll make no progress. I've already told a number of people about her, and I think she'll be a lot busier than she expects. Besides, there's nothing wrong with her recognizing all the potential here."

Why did it sound as though there were layers of meaning in that statement he was missing?

Before he could question his grandmother further, she turned away, adding, "Now go change into proper shoes, or you'll make us late."

When Miss Pearl used that tone, no one in their right mind disobeyed, especially not her family, so Kiah headed back to his room, still contemplating her words.

She was on the wrong track, he knew. His sole intent on getting Mina to come to St. Eustace was to bring her back to life, give her something to do other than sit around, depressed and wallowing. Once she got back on her feet and was ready to go on with her life, there was no way she was staying here.

There was nothing on their quiet island that would hold her, once she got her head straight. Mina was a creature of the city, used to the bustle and noise, not to mention the frenetic activity of a large, major teaching hospital. She'd had an active social life, too, mostly thanks to Warren the Worm's determination to make a name for himself in Toronto's legal circles. The slower pace of St. Eustace wouldn't hold her interest for long.

Kiah was sure of that.

What was important now was helping Mina come to some kind of peace with the loss of her hand. Kiah had watched her, listened to her, and wasn't fooled by the happy face she was showing the world. Even without her breakdown when he'd arrived at her apartment, he'd have known. Sometimes, when she didn't realize he was watching, he saw her agony of spirit in the downturned lips and shadowed eyes, and he wanted to grab her, hold her, tell it would all work out.

But he knew better than to shatter the illusion she tried so hard to keep up, since doing so would make her retreat, probably all the way back to Canada. Mina always had to feel in control—of herself, her world. Losing her hand, and that sorry excuse for a husband, had shaken her confidence, and he wanted to help her get it back.

He'd also done a lot of research since her accident, wanting to be able to offer all the support and assistance she could possibly need. In his estimation, she hadn't gone through a proper mourning period. Instead, she'd used the excuse of Warren and his crap to push her feelings about the loss of her hand and her job aside, bottling it up inside.

Unless and until she could reconcile herself to her new reality, she'd be stuck. And while getting her back into the hospital setting would be good, he wasn't sure how sitting in on the upcoming meeting would help. It would no doubt be dry and somewhat boring.

At least, he thought, as he heard her leave her room and walk down the corridor toward the front door and rose to follow, it would get her out of the house for a while.

Getting her out of her funk would probably be a lot harder.

Having hoped to put off any talk of going to the hospital to sign papers, at least for a few days, Mina had jumped at the chance of being included in the meeting. She'd ignored Kiah's narrow-eyed look in her direction when she agreed to Miss Pearl's suggestion, and now made sure to walk with the older lady, avoiding whatever comments he was planning to make.

Just being in the hospital had brought a rush of longing to prickle the backs of her eyes. Once upon a time, this would have been her milieu, a place she'd feel completely comfortable in. Now the bustle and scents of the hospital were somehow alien. Like wearing a piece of clothing you used to love, which had shrunk in the dryer and just didn't fit properly anymore.

The minister of health's eyebrows rose when Mina was introduced to her.

"Nice to meet you, Dr. Haraldson," she said, giving Mina's hand a firm shake. "I've heard a lot about you, and I'm happy you've decided to lend your expertise to our efforts regarding the Clinicians' Union over the next month."

Mina had to resist turning to glare at Kiah. Obviously, he'd made her participation out to be a done deal and, since she prided herself on her reliability, she was now well and truly trapped for at least a month. It could be longer, depending on what exactly they needed her to do. She wasn't one to leave a job half done.

But there was nothing for it but to smile at the minister and say, "It's my pleasure, Minister Barrows." But as soon as the minister turned to go to her chair at the head of the table, Mina sent Kiah a look that promised retribution.

He responded with the sweetest of smiles, which just annoyed her even more.

"As you all know, there have been several cases of chikungunya reported on Trinidad," Minister Barrows said. "And we need to make sure we're doing everything possible to try to protect St. Eustace from a similar outbreak."

"We haven't had a major outbreak of a vector-borne disease on the island since the early 1990s," Miss Pearl said, obviously for Mina's sake. "Although there has been an increase in cases, year over year, for the past five years."

The representative from the Public Health division nodded, adding, "We have an ongoing program of public service announcements aimed at reminding citizens how to minimize the mosquito population, and be mindful of being bitten. So far, they seem to be effective."

As the meeting went on, Mina was surprised at how interested she became. The minister spoke about their reluctance to restart a fogging program, since it was hard on wildlife and people who had any weakness of the lungs. Then she grilled everyone on how they could beef up the existing mosquito eradication program. When all that was suggested was an increase in the frequency of the public service announcements on the television and radio, Mina found herself interjecting.

"How old are the announcements?"

Minister Barrows wrinkled her brow and turned her gaze to the public health officer, who shrugged slightly and replied, "I believe they were developed either during or just after the 1992 dengue fever outbreak."

"Why do you ask?" The minister looked back at Mina, that slight frown still in place.

"Well, you might want to consider doing a new set of PSAs, if the ones you're using are almost thirty years old."

The scowl intensified. "Why?"

"If you think about it, you have an entire generation—those younger than thirty—who don't know what a major outbreak entails, and probably aren't as cautious as they should be. Couple that with announcements so old that people probably don't even listen to them anymore, and you have a recipe for the type of apathy that could derail your efforts."

There were a few moments of silence while everyone considered her words, and Mina felt heat gathering at the back of her neck. Did they think she was talking nonsense?

Then the minister shook her head, still scowling, although slightly less ferociously.

"I see your point, Dr. Haraldson, but unfortunately our yearly budget won't stretch to new announcements."

Kiah leaned forward and said, "Now that I think about it, that thirty-and-under demographic might not even be watching local television or listening to the radio very much. Even if you don't have the funds for new TV and radio announcements, you should, at the very least, put something out on the social media platforms they *are* tuned into."

"It would be much less expensive," Mina said, backing him up. "And how about the schools? What kind of outreach are you doing there?"

"None that I know of," Miss Pearl replied. "But the district nurses go into the schools regularly, so it wouldn't be difficult to come up with a plan to add to the usual talks we give."

"Getting the young people involved could have a huge impact," Kiah said with a wry smile. "As a parent, I know how much children love to be able to take their parents to task over things."

They all chuckled, even Minister Barrows, who said, "I concur. My sons are in their teens now, and convinced I know nothing worthwhile."

"How about some kind of contest in the schools, to tie in with the district nurses' lectures?" Mina suggested. "Something to get them talking, debating the possibilities?"

That led to a spirited discussion, and a number of ideas were floated, none of which seemed to strike the right chord.

Then Mina had a brainstorm.

"Are the kids here like the ones in Canada, where most of them have cellular phones?"

Once more everyone focused on her, and Miss Pearl replied, "Almost all of them. It's the bane of us older people's existence. You can hardly get them to hear you, much less listen half the time."

"Then, let's kill two birds with one stone," Mina said, excited by her idea.

Kiah started laughing, and she knew he understood exactly what she was thinking, even before he said, "A video competition?"

"Yes." She couldn't help beaming at him. "Let them produce the PSAs. All the phones nowadays have pretty good video capabilities, and I think we'll be surprised at the ingenuity the children will display."

"And any quality issues could probably be cleaned up by the graphics folks," Kiah added. "It will make people sit up and take notice, as well as get the kids fired up."

The air of sudden excitement in the room was exhilarating as she and Kiah batted ideas back and forth, with comments and questions from the other meeting members. By the time they wrapped up, the proposal seemed set to go forward.

"I think we have something worthwhile here," the minister said, with no small measure of satisfaction. "Thank you all for your input, and I'll keep you all informed as we initiate these new ideas."

The meeting was adjourned, and Mina got up and stretched.

The minister paused on her way to the door and said, "Thank you for participating, Dr. Haraldson. This may not be your area of expertise, but I can already see you'll be a valuable resource going forward. Sometimes a fresh perspective is more useful than empirical knowledge."

"Thank you, too, Minister, for letting me sit in on the meeting. It was very interesting."

"You're welcome." Then she looked from Mina to Kiah, and back again. "You two make a good team."

"Don't they?"

Miss Pearl's tone was brisk, as usual, but for some reason Mina felt a little wave of heat rise into her face.

Kiah just laughed.

"That's what comes when you've known a person for an unconscionable length of time. You start reading their mind."

"Whatever the reason, I'm grateful for it," said Minister Barrows, heading for the exit, her little entourage trailing behind her, shedding farewells as they went.

"Don't just stand there," Miss Pearl said when it was just the three of them left in the room. "Take Mina and show her around the hospital."

Kiah held up his hand, stopping the elderly lady before she could say anything more.

"Granny, that can wait. I'm still on vacation, and fully intend to make the most of it before I'm back on call Sunday night. I'm taking Mina to the beach. Do you want a drive home?"

Miss Pearl surrendered far easier than Mina expected. Only with the tightening of her lips did she show any signs of displeasure.

"No," she replied, giving Kiah one of her dry looks. "I'll take a cab when I'm ready."

Mina kept pace with Kiah, but tension tightened her shoulders and she was clenching her teeth as they left the building and approached the car. Finally, unable to bear the thought anymore, she stopped. Kiah took another step before he realized she was no longer walking, and turned a questioning expression her way.

"I don't want to go to the beach." Even being shown around the hospital, although also stress-inducing, was preferable to the thought of putting on a bathing suit or sitting in the heat with a long-sleeved shirt on.

Kiah's eyebrows rose.

"Why not? You love the sea."

The anger that stormed through her system was stronger than she could control, and she glared at him. He knew exactly why she didn't want to go but seemed determined to make her say it.

She stepped closer, almost got into his face, and said, "I don't want people staring at me. I don't want to have to answer when some nosy person asks what happened to my hand. And, most of all, I don't want anyone's pity."

Kiah's expression turned stony, his lips momentarily firming into a hard line before he replied, "The only person pitying you is yourself."

Anger turned to rage in a flash, sending a blaze of fire into her veins, and she clenched her hand into a fist, raising it, ready to throw a punch for the first time in her life. Kiah grabbed her wrist, firm fingers even hotter than her fury-heated skin.

"Dr. K!" A breathless female voice came from behind her, breaking them apart. "Dr. K. Wait."

Mina was gasping, trying to regain her composure. She rubbed her wrist, which almost burned with the sensation of his fingers lingering there, and kept her back turned as someone ran up to where they were standing. Kiah, damn him, looked as cool and unruffled as a bucolic stream, making Mina even angrier.

"Yes, Nurse? What can I do for you?"

"Dr. Golding is asking you not to leave." The nurse must have run all the way, her words coming out in little rushes of air. "We have a patient coming in, and he's asking Dr. Haraldson to assist in his care."

And just like that, Mina's fury morphed to cold, nausea-inducing fear.

CHAPTER FIVE

SHE FROZE.

Heart pounding so hard it made her light-headed, she was barely able to make out what the nurse was saying.

"Scuba diver... Accident... Speargun spear through the thigh... Coming in by ambulance from Barefoot Bay."

That much she gathered. The rest was lost, drowned out by the buzzing in her ears.

What did the doctor think she could do to help? Since the accident, she hadn't seen a patient, hadn't treated or even diagnosed an injury. Without her left hand, she was useless. Why couldn't everyone come to terms with that, the way she had?

"Mina." She came to when strong hands closed on her shoulders, and Kiah's gentle voice broke through the stinging noise in her head. "Mina, the ambulance will be here any minute. We need to go get ready."

"I... I can't, Kiah." The words croaked out, just making it past the jagged ball of terror in her throat. "I can't help."

He gave her a little shake, and his voice took

on that stubborn, take-no-guff tone she knew all too well. "Of course you can help. You're a doctor. That's what we do. And John Golding is young, inexperienced. If he needs help, how can you turn your back on him and the patient?"

"But without my hand..."

He gave her another gentle shake.

"Mina, you lost a hand, not your brain. Don't you know how valuable the experience, the knowledge you have in your head is?"

The question drew her up, made her think, forced her to focus on Kiah's eyes, the strength and confidence in his gaze.

And she drew on what she saw there, knowing he was right, even in the midst of her fear.

"Okay," she said, although her voice still wavered, and she trembled. "Okay. Let's see what we can do."

"Good girl." Kiah smiled, then bent and lightly kissed her lips. "We can be your hands; you just guide us in what we have to do."

Then he was leading her back into the hospital at a quick walk, as she was trying to forget how wonderful his lips felt against hers, how it was that, not her fears, which was making her heart pound.

She must be losing her mind to even notice such a thing. After all, this was Kiah, and they'd been exchanging platonic kisses like that since they were just kids. Or maybe it was her brain's way of distracting her from what she considered a scary situation.

If that was the case, it was effective, her fear dissipating as soon as she went back through the hospital doors.

The nurse was waiting there and immediately said, "If you'll come with me, Dr. Haraldson, I'll get you some scrubs."

"Thank you," she replied, hurrying after the other woman.

Once she'd changed, the nurse led her back to the emergency room and into a cubicle, just as a siren could be heard in the distance.

The man who approached her looked as though he could still be in high school, although his voice was deep and confident as he said, "Dr. Haraldson, thank you for assisting. I'm John Golding."

She nodded, giving him a slight smile as she went past him to a shelf where the gloves were. "Nice to meet you, Dr. Golding. What can you tell me about the patient?"

"From the ambulance report, the twenty-five-year-old patient, Donovan Exeter, was scuba diving when he was shot through the thigh with a speargun."

"A through-and-through?" she asked.

"No, the spear is still in situ. It entered through

the anterolateral aspect, with the tip and about two inches of the shaft exiting the inner thigh. The paramedics wrapped the leg to keep the projectile as stable as possible."

"Any signs of distal ischemia, pulse deficit or hypotension?"

"No. The limb is warm, both the dorsalis pedis and posterior tibial pulses are strong, and his blood pressure is high, not low. He is also able to move his toes."

While they spoke, Mina had pulled a pair of gloves from the dispenser, and it was only now that she realized she had no way to put them on. Not to mention, no left hand to wear one on. Up until then, she hadn't given a thought to the fact her truncated limb was on display in the scrubs, but now embarrassment threatened to make her walk out. Yet, she could hear the clatter of the gurney and knew the patient was almost there.

Gathering all the poise she could manage, she turned to the nearby nurse and said, "Please assist me in putting on these gloves."

To her surprise, the nurse didn't even blink, but said, "Of course, Doctor."

The nurse held a glove, and Mina slipped her right hand into it. But when it came to the left...

"I doubt it will stay on," the nurse whispered quietly.

The gurney came through the door, Kiah accompanying the paramedics from the bay, and there was no more time to dither.

"Thank you," she said to the nurse, then moved forward to evaluate the patient, sticking her left arm into the pocket of her scrub top. Hopefully, she'd remember to keep it there.

Then it was an exercise in frustration as she was relegated to watching everyone else do the hands-on stuff, while she could only advise.

It quickly became apparent the only way to know how much damage was done to Donovan Exeter's leg was via X-ray.

Mina moved to the head of the bed, to explain to him what was going to happen next.

"Mr. Exeter, we're going to have to do some scans to see how much damage was done to your leg internally, before we attempt to remove the spear."

With the patient's consent in place, he was taken to radiology.

"Do you think he'll need to have an angiogram?" Kiah asked as the three doctors followed the patient. "If so, I'll have to call in the chief radiologist, who's off today."

Mina shook her head. "I'm reasonably sure any vascular damage will be slight, just from the position of the spear, and his ankle/brachial index is well above danger level. There's also no signs the femur was damaged, but we'll find out for sure after the X-rays."

And to her satisfaction, she was correct, although there was no way to know absolutely what they'd find when the spear was removed. In cases like this one, the embedded projectile put pressure on the wound from the inside, often staunching bleeding from damaged veins and arteries. It was only when that pressure was released that they'd know for sure what needed to be repaired.

At the last minute, she balked at going into the operating room.

"The wound tract looks clear," she whispered to Kiah. "Some moderate hematomas to be evacuated. There's nothing special I can add to the surgery, and I'll just be taking up space."

"I'm letting John do the surgery," he replied. "We'll both supervise. But if anything unusual does come up, I want you there to make sure we do the best we can for the patient."

When she started to object, Kiah held up his hand, stopping her midsentence.

"Donovan Exeter is twenty-five, Mina. Still a young man, hopefully with a lot of years ahead of him. The least we can do is ensure he has full use of his leg, not take the chance he's maimed because of a silly accident like this one."

Mina turned away so he couldn't see the

gleam of tears in her eyes. What he said was right, and hit home with a blow straight to her heart. No one should have their life, or livelihood, curtailed because of an accident.

"Okay," she said, proud when her voice came out normal, not strained or trembling. "I'll go scrub in. And I have to figure out what to do with this damn stump. I can't wear a glove on it, and the sock isn't sterile."

The last part came out fierce and strong, annoyance sweeping the last of her uncertainty away, and giving her a new, albeit strange, problem to focus on.

"Hey," he said, putting a hand on her shoulder. "We'll work it out, okay?"

"Sure. Sure," she muttered, stalking off toward the surgical ward, feeling his hand fall away, although the sensation of the pressure and comfort it afforded lingered.

Kiah watched for Mina to come into the scrubbing area, and when she stepped through the doors, already capped, masked and wearing disposable booties, her body language spoke volumes. Here was a woman who wished herself anywhere but where she was.

He was about to go to offer her help with scrubbing in, when a nurse stepped to Mina's side and said, "Can I assist you, Dr. Haraldson?"

"Please," Mina replied, her tone cool and controlled. "And thank you."

The nurse put on her nonsterile apron and then did a thorough job of scrubbing her hand and arm.

Kiah paused on his way into the gowning area and said, "I'll gown up, then help you with yours."

"Thank you."

Anyone who didn't know her would think her response merely polite, but Kiah wasn't fooled. Mina was hating every moment of the situation. She was one of the most self-sufficient and capable people he knew, and having to let someone else help her do something that had become second nature for her must sting.

It was all he could do not to send her a sympathetic glance, but he restrained himself. One hint of kindly concern would just make her even more annoyed and self-conscious.

Yet, for all his worry, she handled the gowning and gloving better than he'd expected, telling the nurse to let her try opening the gown and putting it on herself.

"After all, I'm going to have to get used to doing this, aren't I? In an emergency, no one has time to be fiddling around, helping me."

With an expert flick of her hand, she got the gown partially open and stuck her left arm in.

Then Kiah held his breath, watching from the corner of his eye as she used that arm to shake the fabric, trying to get the right armhole open.

"There," she said as she pushed her right arm in, and she might as well have danced a jig, too, she sounded so elated. "That worked better than I expected."

"Me, too," he admitted, sending her a grin, which, although hidden behind his mask, was probably unmistakable. Once the nurse had tied the gown, he said, "Now for the gloves. Have you decided how to handle them?"

"As usual," she said, the challenge in her voice unmistakable. "I'm not operating, so the floppy fingers won't matter, and my forearm and gown should keep it on."

"Aye, aye, Captain," he replied, and was rewarded with a distinct glare from her already flashing brown eyes.

Then they were joined by John Golding, and once he had scrubbed in, they entered the operating room.

Mina had been right about the extent of the injuries, and when the spear was removed, there was little work to be done, except for the evacuation of the clots.

"Watch his blood pressure," Mina told the anesthesiologist. "That would be one of the first signs that we missed vascular damage."

Kiah was enchanted, watching her in theater for the first time. As soon as she'd stepped through the door, all signs of self-consciousness or annoyance disappeared, and she was all business. Yet, in spite of being the specialist, she let John set the pace, only answering his questions, not telling him what to do unless he asked.

And despite Kiah's best intentions, his determination not to cut her any slack because he felt sorry for her, his heart ached, knowing that from now on, hers would be only a supporting role.

It made him want to rage, to bargain with God, to cry. He'd give his own hand if she could have hers back.

"Great job, Dr. Golding," Mina said as the young doctor was applying the negative pressure bandage. "You've got good hands."

John looked up, his eyes gleaming. "And thank you, Dr. Haraldson, for guiding me so expertly."

By the time they met up again, once more in street clothes, Mina looked a totally different person. Euphoric. Grinning.

"That went well," she said as they headed for the car. "There were a couple of times I wanted to grab the instruments and do it myself, but it wasn't as horrible as I thought it would be."

"Is this where I get to say I told you so? Because you know I'll be all over that," Kiah responded, earning himself a swat on his arm.

"Don't you dare."

"You're a natural-born teacher," he said. "I didn't realize how good until I saw you in action."

Mina shrugged. "I've never had a problem instructing others. I guess that's why Toronto South asked if I'd consider staying on as a lecturer. I said no, because I couldn't fathom not having my own practice, or being unable to operate anymore."

Shock brought Kiah to a halt. "They offered to have you stay on, and you refused?"

Mina kept walking, not even looking back as she replied, "Yep. Couldn't see it happening."

But she probably could now, Kiah realized, his heart sinking at the thought of her leaving even sooner than he expected she would.

CHAPTER SIX

THAT EVENING, AFTER DINNER, Miss Pearl said, "The two of you should go out, since you didn't get to go to the beach this afternoon."

"I was planning to help Charm with her homework," Kiah said.

Mina knew he'd felt a little guilty, being away and leaving all the parenting chores to Miss Pearl, but the old lady just flapped her hand at him.

"She did it at Mrs. Gordon's house this afternoon, and I checked it when she got home. Besides, it's Friday night. She deserves a little rest from schoolwork."

"And Granny said she and I could watch a movie tonight," Charm added.

Kiah wrinkled his nose. "One of those sappy romances the two of you love so much?"

Charm turned to Mina and said, "I don't know why you hang out with him, Auntie. He doesn't know the first thing about romance."

"Oh, really?" Kiah narrowed his eyes at his niece in mock anger. "I'll have you know I'm very romantic."

"I'll ask your girlfriend," came the pert reply. "If you ever get one."

Mina almost choked with mirth, and even Miss Pearl seemed hard-pressed to stop herself from laughing. Though the old lady had the wherewithal to reprimand her great-granddaughter for sassing her uncle, she also had to press her lips tight to stop from joining in with Mina's laughter.

Kiah pounced, tackling Charm on the couch, tickling her and saying, "Apologize to your favorite uncle!"

"My only uncle!" she shrieked while laughing, trying to avoid his fingers, which had unerringly found her ribs.

Eventually, Miss Pearl said, "That's enough, Hezekiah. You'll make the child throw up."

"Ah, sah," he said, flopping back against the couch cushions and tugging a still-giggling Charm against his side. "You see what I have to put up with?"

Charm laid her head on his chest and snuggled in close. "Uncle, how come you didn't pick me up at school today? I thought you would."

"Auntie Mina and I had to help with an operation at the hospital."

"Oh. That's cool, but I didn't think you'd be back at work so soon."

Mina could hear the disappointment in the

young girl's voice, but there was no reproach in her tone. The two of them there, together, looked perfect, and Mina felt a warm, sweet glow watching the interplay. Kiah may have fallen into parenthood through tragedy, but it was obvious he was doing a good job of it.

"I didn't plan to be, but I got called in unexpectedly. How was school?"

"Good. We have a new boy in class. His name is Ramesh, and he just moved here from India. The other kids laughed when they heard his name, but I told them not to. Told them that our names probably sound weird to him, too."

The correlation between what Charm described and Mina's first meeting with Kiah was unmistakable, and the wave of nostalgia sweeping through her made Mina smile.

Then Kiah looked up, his gaze colliding with hers, and in his gleaming eyes she saw something she'd never seen before. Something powerful and raw that stole her breath and turned the previous warm glow to heat, which raced out from her belly into her bloodstream.

Time slowed, stopped. Everything faded away, leaving just her and Kiah, caught in a moment for which there were no words, no explanation easily found.

Still holding Mina's gaze, Kiah dipped his head and kissed Charm's hair.

"My sweetheart," he murmured. "That's the most beautiful thing you could do."

Mina looked away first, unable to hold that intense gaze a moment more.

Shaken, she got up, saying, "If we're going out, I should shower and change."

As Mina got to the passageway leading to the bedrooms, she heard Charm ask, "Are you really going out, Uncle Kiah?"

It made her pause, waiting to hear what was said. While she got no sense that Charm resented her, Mina could understand why she might not want her uncle to go back out. After all, not only had he not picked her up from school that day, but he'd also just got back from his trip to Canada.

"Don't you want me to?" Kiah asked in return.

"Yes, I do want you to. If you stay here, you'll just make rude comments and ruin the good parts of the movie."

Chuckling quietly to herself, Mina continued on her way, as Kiah appealed to Miss Pearl for help.

"Granny, are you going to let her talk to me that way?"

"Huh. I'd chastise her, but we all know is the truth she's talking."

But by the time Mina got to her bedroom and

closed the door behind her, her amusement had faded, and anxiety took over.

Going out was the last thing she wanted to do. Sure, she been elated earlier at being back in the operating room. Remembering, on a visceral, soul-deep level, why she'd become a doctor, and knowing for the first time since the accident she'd find a way to be true to her calling.

It was a little like awakening from a deep, restless sleep, with the sense of time lost, she thought, as she climbed into the shower.

But that was the hospital. A place where no one working there would be inclined to be curious about a one-handed person. Anywhere else, she was sure to get those strange looks and stares, the inquisitive questions.

Yet, hiding from it wasn't going to change anything, and that reality was something she'd steadfastly refused to accept.

Caring for the patient today had brought it into focus. She was in a state of transition from the life she used to have, to a new way of being. Looking back, she wondered where things had gone wrong, and why she'd made some of the decisions she'd made. But in truth, no amount of navel-gazing was going to change a moment of her past and, in order to go forward, she had to find acceptance.

Lifting her left arm, she looked at her stump,

turning it back and forth under the water. Seeing and examining it fully for the first time. She'd been trying to ignore it, to pretend that at some point she'd look down and her hand would, magically, be there.

So much denial, and anger, and sadness, over something no one—nothing—could undo.

Tears threatened, but she held them back, despite the fact she felt only a lingering sense of sorrow, not the racking pain she associated with thoughts of the accident and memories of her loss.

"It's time you got your head on straight, Mina Haraldson." The words echoed in the shower stall, weightier for being spoken aloud. "No more feeling sorry for yourself or pretending that losing your hand means everything is finished. Time to make a new plan and get on with life."

Then she stuck her head under the spray, letting the water wash away the tears she swore would be the last she shed for Warren, for the accident, for the loss of her hand. For a life that had, if she were honest, grown stale and gray despite her love for her work.

Onward and upward.

By the time she'd dressed and looked at herself in the mirror, Mina felt she'd successfully covered any evidence of her tears. A little eyeshadow and mascara did wonders, she reflected, and her linen pirate-inspired blouse, with its flouncy cuffs, hopefully would camouflage her stump.

Even her new determination and just-finished pep talk couldn't totally reduce her tension, but seeing Kiah in a bright orange shirt somehow made the outing far less stressful.

"Going for the Bird of Paradise look?" she asked, earning a giggle from Charm and a glare from Kiah.

"Don't you like it?" he asked, striking a pose, one hand behind his head, the other on an outthrust hip. "Will it embarrass you to be seen with me like this?"

"Would you change it, if I said yes?"

"Nope," he said, striding across the room, then doing a dramatic turn. "I'd run downtown and see if I could find a pair of matching pants."

"You see how bad he is, Auntie?" Charm said, shaking her head.

"Oh, you'd be surprised at how many ladies love a man in a blinding shirt," Mina replied, making even Miss Pearl chuckle.

In truth, the shirt emphasized Kiah's handsomeness, showing off his dark, smooth complexion and sparkling eyes. As he kissed first Miss Pearl then Charm good-night, Mina found herself hard-pressed to take her gaze off him. The effect of the look he'd given her earlier lin-

gered beneath her skin, heightening her awareness of him. No matter how often she told herself
it was just a sweet, nostalgic moment, her body
refused to listen. Instead, she was extremely
conscious of their closeness within the confines
of the car as they got underway.

But she made sure to keep the conversation
light, hoping these new sensations would fade.

They better.

Kiah found himself watching Mina carefully as
they left the house.

He wasn't sure what had passed between them
earlier, when he'd reacted to Charm's story. His
niece's words had taken him back to the first
time they'd met, and his gaze was drawn straight
to Mina's.

The memory had been there in her eyes, too,
but it had been soft, fond, while he...

Hell, he didn't even know what he'd been pro-
jecting, only knew the raw emotion in his blood
wasn't soft. Or fond. No, it had been fierce, almost desperate. And God only knew what Mina
thought his expression meant.

He half expected her to bring it up, but she
didn't. Instead, she chatted about Miss Pearl and
Charm's movie date, as though that was the only
thing of importance occurring that evening.

It was a relief.

When they pulled up to the little club on the beach, she gave a cry of delight.

"I remember this place," she said as she opened her car door. "It wasn't called the Sweet Spot then, though, was it?"

"No," he replied, smiling at her enthusiasm. "It was called Yellow Bird the last time you were here."

"We had a blast that night, although that young woman who took a shine to American Jimmy got so drunk and became obnoxious when he wouldn't take her home with him. Whatever happened to Jimmy?" she asked as they approached the door. "Is he still around? He's a fun guy."

"He is still around," Kiah said, of the man who'd come to work on St. Eustace fifteen years before and never left. "He's been seeing a really nice woman, and I heard he's gone to Barbados to meet her family."

"Sounds serious," she said as she looked around the small club. In true Caribbean style, it was still almost empty, since most people came out later. It was a nice night, warm, with a hint of sea breeze, so they wound their way through the tables to the other door, which led to the patio.

There they found a table near the railing, within eyeshot of the sea lapping on the nearby rocks. Once they sat down, Kiah continued the conversation.

"Apparently he's asked her to marry him."

"I'm a little surprised. Wasn't he the local Romeo?"

Kiah chuckled. "Once Jimmy met Sharon, that was it. You can tell from just seeing them together how in love with her he is."

Mina turned her gaze toward the water, a pensive expression flitting over her face for an instant, making him wonder what she was thinking. But before he could ask, she faced him again and said, "Charm was asking me about Karlene last night, after dinner."

His heart rate kicked up in reaction to her words, and he scrubbed his palm along his cheek, getting his emotions under control, before asking, "What did she say?"

"Just asked me what I meant when I said she reminded me of her mother. Wanted to know if I liked Karlene. Things like that. She said neither you nor Miss Pearl like to talk about her, and I think she needs you to."

The weight in his heart increased, grew almost unbearable for a moment. Then he took a deep breath, trying to regain his equilibrium. When Mina reached across the table to take his hand in hers, Kiah hung on to it, as though it were a lifeline.

"We used to, when she first came to us, but every time we mentioned Karlene's name or said something about her, Charm shut down. Granny and I agreed to stop, figuring when Charm was ready to talk about her mother, she'd let us know. Ask questions. I think, somewhere along the line, not talking about her turned into a habit."

She squeezed his fingers a little tighter.

"Well, discuss it with Miss Pearl, and the two of you come up with a plan. It's been five years since Karlene and Roy died. Maybe Charm has questions she needs answered. Not just about her mom, but about what happened."

He shook his head, unable to help it. The last thing he wanted was to have to discuss her parents' murder-suicide with Charm, but in his gut he knew he'd have to.

"She needs to know why it happened, Kiah. Charm probably hates her father, which is only natural under the circumstances. No doubt you do, too, in some ways. But the difference is, half of her comes from Roy. She needs to understand what happened."

"I still don't fully understand it, Mina." His throat felt raw, just as it had the night after the phone had rung, and a police constable had called from Canada to inform him Karlene and Roy were dead. Then, though, it was because he'd roared in anguish, unable to restrain himself, mindless with grief. Now it was because he knew he'd have to relive it, sometime soon, for Charm's sake.

Mina stroked the back of his hand with her thumb, as though trying to soothe him as best she could. It helped, but not enough to make the conversation palatable.

"Roy was suffering from PTSD. You know that."

"But how do you explain that to a twelve-year-old?"

"Charm is more than mature enough to hear the truth. That her father went off to war one man and came back another. That he tried to get help, but it wasn't enough."

Now anger edged the fear and sadness aside, and he welcomed it. "Do I tell her that her grand-mother, who's a bitter, controlling woman, couldn't stop stirring up trouble? Tell her that her poor father, already fighting the demons in his head, couldn't take any more of his mother-in-law's nagging and bickering? Does she get to hear that part, too? Because I can't even say it without feeling ill."

"No," Mina said softly, her eyes full of gentle wisdom and care. "She doesn't need to know that part. That's more than is necessary right now. But she does need to know her father wasn't a monster, which means she's not half monster too, if you see what I mean?"

"I do see what you mean," he said, the reluctance clear in his tone. He, better than anyone else, recognized the effect knowing you had a monstrous parent could have on a child. Then he shook his head, his lips twisting to the side for an instant. "But why is everything so difficult, Mina? Why can't life be simple?"

"I wish I knew, Kiah. I really do."

Just then the waiter approached and Mina let go of his hand, leaving him suddenly hollow and bereft.

CHAPTER SEVEN

SHE'D WANTED A change of subject, away from American Jimmy and his new girlfriend, but going from that to Karlene and Roy, and Kiah having to talk to Charm about them, left her raw. Both were subjects that made her heartache all the harder to bear, albeit in different ways.

Not that she was bitter, really; she wished nothing but the best for Jimmy and his lady. But hearing about them falling in love was a reminder of how unlikely it was that she'd ever be in a similar situation. Warren and his ugly truths had put paid to that.

Then talking about Karlene and Roy... *Ouch.*

She'd been the one Kiah called, after hearing from the cops, and it was Mina who'd gone to the police station to be with Charm. The memory was one that haunted her still, and she could only imagine how Kiah felt about having to relive that time with his niece.

So, having the waiter come to take their drink orders was something of a relief.

"Rum punch?" Kiah questioned, after the waiter left. "You remember how strong those are, right?"

Mina gave him a grin and nodded. "Yep, but I feel like celebrating, and I know you'll take care of me if I get a little tipsy."

The club started filling up, and people gravitated to their table. A couple of men, whom Kiah introduced to her as Slim and Henkel—she never did get their real names—were the ones who stuck around, while others came and went. They were fun, trading jokes and stories with Kiah while flirting outrageously with Mina, who laughed it all off.

"Hey, why you so nosy, Henkel?" Kiah broke in to the conversation, as his friend started questioning Mina about her life.

"Cho, man. Just trying to get to know this lovely lady a little better," came the easy reply, accompanied by a sly grin. "I think your *friend* is old enough to take care of herself. You mind your own business."

"On that note," Mina said, laughing as she got up, "I'm going to the ladies' room."

There was no way she was hanging around for the part when he asked her what happened to her hand.

She'd seen the men glancing at her empty sleeve whenever she raised her arm above the level of the table, and knew it was coming. If she could forestall it until after she'd had another rum punch, maybe she could come up with a witty, pithy reply.

There was a bit of a line for the bathroom, and by the time she came back outside it was to find the dance floor crowded with people, all jumping and dancing to a popular calypso song. And there, in the midst of it all, was Kiah.

Mina kept walking, even though her first impulse was to stop and stare. The woman dancing with him was gorgeous, with long, professionally streaked hair, impeccable makeup and an hourglass figure on full display in a tight, skimpy jumpsuit.

And if she danced any closer to Kiah, they'd be wearing the same pants.

Why that annoyed Mina as much as it did, she didn't want to contemplate, but it took everything she had to keep a slight smile on her face and not look back at the gyrating couple.

Slim and Henkel got up as she approached, and Henkel held out his hand. Then he did a little sideways shimmy toward the dance floor.

"Come dance with me, Mina," he said.

She laughed and shook her head, already lowering herself into her chair. Thankfully it was facing away from the dance floor, so she could avoid the display going on there.

With an elaborate sigh, Henkel sat down beside her and, resting his elbow on the table, put his chin in his palm so he was looking right into her face.

"So, Miss Mina, how long are you staying here with me?"

He made it sound as though she came specifically to see him, and would be moving into his house any minute, and she couldn't help chuckling.

"I'm not sure yet. Probably about a month. Just until I get the new systems I'll be working on for the hospital squared away."

How a man of his age could still achieve puppy-dog eyes was a mystery to Mina, but somehow he managed it.

"If you need someone to show you around and take you to nicer places than this, just let me know, you hear?"

Slim kissed his teeth and rolled his eyes, then leaned forward so he was almost right between Mina and his friend.

"Don't go anywhere with him. You don't need an old reprobate like him hanging around."

"Who you calling a reprobate?" Henkel abandoned his attempt at flirtation and rounded on his friend.

"You, same one," was the reply.

"Huh. If I'm so much of a reprobate, how come you're always hanging out with me?"

"Because I'm one, too," was the response. "But I'm just honest about it."

Mina couldn't help laughing at the banter, even though her thoughts remained fixed on the dance floor. The song had changed, but Kiah hadn't come back.

As though reading her mind, Slim looked that way and shook his head, before taking a sip of his drink.

"Aii, sah. That Trini girl goin' wine off Kiah's pants front, if he's not careful."

"We used to call him 'Calypso Kiah' back at university," Mina said, trying to sound nonchalant, and steadfastly resisting the urge to turn around to gawk, too.

"Not surprised," Henkel replied, his eyes narrowing, so that Mina wondered exactly what was happening. "You knock two tin cans together on the other side of the island, and that man is there to dance. *Whew*, that woman getting on bad."

"Getting on bad" was one of those all-purpose expressions Mina had learned over years of knowing Kiah. It could mean anything, from praise of the woman's dancing skills to her being about to start a fight, but somehow she didn't think Henkel meant the latter. His eyes were wide, and he raised a hand to fan at his face.

Slim chuckled. "Niesha's been trying to reel

Kiah in for the last six months, not realizing she hasn't set the hook yet."

Henkel shook his head. "Lost cause, that man. She could hook me, reel me in and sink me, all in that time, and I wouldn't even mind."

"Ha, that's what you say now, but Niesha would chew you up and spit you out without blinking, and if she ever looks at you the way she looking at Kiah now, you'd run *so* fast."

Okay, now Mina had to glance over her shoulder to see what it was the men were looking at, and when she did, she wished she hadn't.

With her body pressed flush to Kiah's and one arm draped over his shoulder, Niesha was staring up into his face with an expression of blatant hunger. And that swivel thing she was doing with her hips…

With heat rising at her nape, Mina forced herself to turn back around and reached for her glass, trying to push away the emotions bubbling in her chest. It wasn't as though she wasn't used to seeing women throw themselves at Kiah. That had been happening since they hit puberty and the girls started noticing how handsome he was. Yet, somehow, tonight was different.

It actually *hurt*.

She took a long swallow of her drink and tried to focus on what the other men were saying. And by the time Kiah made his way back to the table,

Niesha in tow, Mina thought she'd got her inexplicable jealousy under control.

"Whew, that was something, boy." Niesha sank into a chair and flipped her hair back over one shoulder, giving Kiah a sultry glance as he sat next to her. "You know how to move, man."

Kiah just laughed, glancing at Mina, who quirked her eyebrows at him, trying not to show him her teeth, the way she wanted to.

"Niesha, this is my friend Mina. Mina, this is Niesha."

"Hi," Niesha said with a grin, but Mina thought her eyes were watchful. "You're Kiah's friend from Canada, right?"

"Yes," Mina said, smiling in return, although it was the last thing she felt like doing.

"I don't know how you stand the cold up there. I like things *hot*."

The look she gave Kiah made it obvious she considered him one of those hot things she liked.

"It's not so bad when you get used to it," Kiah said, sending Mina a mischievous grin. "Although Mina always complained all through winter, and she was born there."

Mina made a blah-blah-blah motion with her hand back at him, which made him laugh, then Niesha leaned toward him, pressing her ample bosom against his arm.

"While I remember, I'm putting together a team for the bank's fund-raising 5K run. Join me?"

And after that Niesha dominated the conversation, leaving Mina mostly to her own thoughts, since they were talking about places and people she didn't know. And when Kiah tried to draw her into the conversation, she resisted, albeit with a smile, unaccountably annoyed with him, although he'd really done nothing wrong.

Kiah glanced at his watch and decided to call it a night. He'd had more than enough of Niesha, who was loud, brassy and handsy, too. She'd dragged him onto the dance floor while he was on his way to the bar, and, as hard as he tried to keep a decent distance between them, she'd been all over him like polyester on a humid day.

Normally he didn't think twice about dancing that way. But since Niesha had made it clear on several occasions that she was willing to have an intimate relationship with him, and Kiah wasn't interested, it didn't feel right to encourage her.

Worse, once back at the table, she'd totally taken over, hardly giving anyone else a chance to get a word in edgewise. He'd been unable to resist making the comparison between her and Mina, who didn't need to slather on makeup or wear a barely-there outfit to be beautiful. And although she'd consumed a number of rum punches, Mina hadn't gotten loud or boisterous, nor demanded the attention of everyone at the table be focused on her.

Even though he thought Mina was still too slender, he preferred her more subtle curves— her delicacy—to Niesha's buxom figure.

But he was going to have to have some sharp words with Henkel, who was hanging all over Mina as if he was about to smother her. Not that Mina seemed to particularly mind, since she just laughed and had a joking reply to most of his advances.

Kiah didn't know why seeing the other man whispering in Mina's ear made him so annoyed, but it definitely had to stop.

As soon as he said they were leaving, both Niesha and Henkel objected, but Kiah didn't bother arguing with them. Instead he put his arm around Mina's shoulders and, with a last round of goodbyes, led her out of the club.

"You can stay, if you want," she said, once they were outside. "No need to leave on my account."

Kiah paused. "Did you want to stay?"

"No, but I can grab a cab home, if you wanted to go back in. Niesha seemed very disappointed that you were leaving so soon."

Kiah started walking again, tugging Mina along with him, his arm still over her shoulders. She was walking steadily, but he'd seen how many rum punches she'd drunk, and wasn't taking any chances. The unpaved, gravel-covered parking lot was uneven. "I can't help that. Besides, I'm really not interested in her."

"She's very beautiful."

Kiah snorted. "Not my type."

They'd gotten to the car but before he could open her door, Mina turned her back to it, blocking the handle. "Kiah, when was the last time you had a relationship?"

She knew the answer, he was sure, but he replied anyway. "Not since Valerie and I broke up. Why?"

She didn't reply to his question, just tilted her head to one side, her shadowed gaze searching his. In the faint light from the street, which cast her cheekbones and tender lips into sharp relief and made her eyes look wide and alluring, her face was mysterious.

"You never told me what happened between you. You'd sounded happy with her."

Kiah rubbed at his cheek. This was the last thing he wanted to talk about, especially on the heels of their earlier conversation about Karlene and Roy.

"We had a parting of the ways, Mina."

She huffed out a little breath, her lips curving, although she didn't really look amused.

"What caused it, this parting of the ways?"

"We…disagreed on the advisability of my taking custody of Charm. Valerie was very upfront about not wanting to raise another person's child."

"Wow." Mina sounded genuinely shocked. "So what did she think should happen to Charm, then, if you didn't take custody?"

"I don't think she much cared."

Mina scowled. "That's the worst thing I've heard in…in forever. I hope you told her where to get off."

He couldn't help the bitter, rueful bark of pseudo laughter he gave. "I'm afraid I did, and I'm not proud of it. I hadn't lost my temper like that in years."

Mina shook her head, her lips firming for an instant. "You'd just gone through the tragedy of Karlene's death, and were under the stress of your mother and her nonsense. No one could blame you for losing it. Charm's future was at stake."

He blamed himself, though, for the loss of control, for expecting Valerie to be more supportive than she was. "I should have expected her reaction. She'd already told me she wasn't interested in having children at all."

"And you agreed with that? Before this… disagreement?"

Kiah nodded, watching Mina's expression, wondering where she was going with this entire conversation.

"It didn't really matter to me, whether we had kids or not. I actually would have preferred not to. You know I've always said that between my father dying so young and my mom's emotional instability, it's probably better these genes don't get passed on. My thoughts on that haven't changed."

"Even though you've been tested for the congenital condition your father had?"

He noticed she didn't mention his mother and was glad. He didn't want to discuss her if he could help it, nor talk about how much of her he sometimes saw in himself. Like the night he and Valerie got into it, and he'd said some truly hurtful things before walking away, knowing he desperately needed to cool off.

"It's not worth the risk," he said. "I didn't plan on it, but I have Charm to take care of, and that's enough for me."

"Is it really?" She held up her hand, as though knowing his answer already. "Forget I said anything. It's the rum talking. I worry about you, want you to be happy."

"I am." Even as he said it, he realized it was

true, and a lot of his present happiness came from being there just then, with her. "And I want the same for you."

Something changed in her expression. If he didn't know her as well as he did, he'd have missed it, but even so, he couldn't interpret the emotion that suddenly shadowed her eyes and fractionally tightened her lips.

When she reached out and trailed her fingers along his cheek, so lightly they could have been butterfly wings, he froze, startled by the surge of emotion engendered by her tender caress.

"Let me tell you a secret," she said, leaning in so her face was close enough that he could have kissed her, if he dared. "Sometimes it's far easier to accept your limitations than it is to fight against them and get your heart broken."

Before he realized her intention, Mina closed the gap between them and placed her lips on his. Soft and sweet and warm, they teased his mouth, moving ever so slightly, and now he recognized what he was feeling.

Desire.

Need.

But this was Mina.

Mina!

And although he wanted to pull her closer, deepen the kiss into something carnal and fierce, he held himself as still as possible, hardly daring to breathe, lest she figure out what he was feeling.

She pulled back, her gaze searching his, then she turned away, fumbling with the handle of the car door, saying, "Dammit, Kiah. You got me drunk again, and now you won't take me home to bed."

"Lawd," he groaned, hoping she would think he was just grousing and not wishing he could do just that—take her home to his bed, and make love to her all night long.

And he knew she'd interpreted it the way he hoped when she laughed, and would have tumbled headfirst into the car if he hadn't had a firm hold on her arm.

CHAPTER EIGHT

MINA AWOKE ON the morning after Kiah had taken her to the club by the beach, and lay staring at the ceiling, trying to sort through what had happened the night before. It was a complete departure from her usual self, almost beyond comprehension.

Why'd she been jealous of Niesha monopolizing Kiah's time and dancing so erotically with him? It wasn't as though she'd never seen Kiah flirting and dancing with women before. Hell, she'd teased him about his amorous adventures since they were fourteen or fifteen.

But last night had been different. She'd seethed, wanting his attention for herself, not on the beautiful, bountiful Niesha.

And then, if that weren't bad enough, when they were standing in the parking lot, she'd had the overwhelming urge to kiss him, and she had. The jolt of awareness and desire rocketing through her body when their lips touched had made her sudden physical attraction toward him abundantly clear.

Rolling over onto her side, she stared sightlessly at the window.

She wished she could put it down to the rum, but she knew that while she'd been a little tipsy, she was nowhere near drunk enough to use the alcohol as an excuse.

And there'd been no reaction from him to the kiss. Not that she'd expected him to grab her and ravage her on the spot. That would have been ludicrous and hysterical. But wouldn't he have at least tried to kiss her back, if the thought had even fractionally crossed his mind? And when she'd seen his expression afterward, it had been blank, with perhaps a hint of a question in his eyes.

No interest or passion.

Not even a touch.

The entire situation was embarrassing. And confusing.

Where had these feelings even come from?

Sighing, she sat up, since she could clearly hear the rest of the household stirring. Hopefully, Kiah would think nothing of what had happened between them, and look at the kiss as one of their usual friendly salutes. If he brought it up with her, she had no idea how to react, or what to tell him.

Thankfully, he didn't mention it, and everything seemed normal, except for her heightened awareness of his every move.

Kiah came into the kitchen, where she was

helping Miss Pearl fix breakfast, and asked, "Hey, you want to go for a drive after breakfast?"

"Sure," she replied, although wondering if it was a way to get her alone to talk about the night before. Then she turned to Charm. "You coming with us, kiddo?"

Besides the fact that she enjoyed Charm's company, the little girl would be a good buffer between Kiah and herself, until Mina could figure out what was going on inside her own head.

"Yes," was the reply, laced with more eagerness than she'd expected. Then she understood why. "It'll be much better than staying here and reading my history book. I have to do an essay, but it's so boring."

"Wasn't my favorite subject, either," Mina confessed. "But it's important to understand why things in the past happened the way they did. You know the famous quote about forgetting the past, don't you?"

"The one about having to repeat it?" she asked. When Mina nodded, Charm sighed. "Granny says it all the time. Usually when I make the same mistake twice."

"If you're tired of hearing it, then don't make silly mistakes over and over again," was Miss Pearl's tart remark from over at the stove.

Charm wrinkled her nose, and Mina swallowed her chuckle. No sense in letting the old lady know her great-granddaughter was silently sassing her!

"When is your essay due?" Kiah asked.

"Not for two weeks," Charm replied, turning her best begging face to her uncle. "I have lots of time."

"Okay, you can come," he said, continuing over her cry of jubilation, "but I want to see a first draft by the end of next week."

"Can we stop at Salty's and get roast corn?"

"Sure," he said, earning another whoop from Charm.

The day was gorgeous, with just a few puffy clouds drifting overhead in the azure sky and a nice breeze coming off the coast. Port Michael, the capital of St. Eustace, was situated on the southeast side of the island, and Kiah turned the car east, following the road that hugged the coast.

Charm was in high spirits and carried on a running, largely one-sided commentary of the music she liked, TV shows she'd watched, and the latest drama going on at school. Kiah put in an observation or answered when necessary, leaving Mina to follow her own muddled thoughts.

But despite doing her best to appear as if nothing at all had changed, she found herself noticing little things about Kiah that she hadn't really paid attention to for a long time.

The deep, warm timbre of his voice; the rumbling laughter that flowed from him so easily.

How broad his shoulders were, and how the muscles in his arms and legs flexed and relaxed beneath his clothes.

Those sensual hands, with their long fingers and broad palms.

The absolute, breathtaking beauty of his smile, and the way the corners of his eyes crinkled when he was amused.

In a strange way, it was like seeing him anew, all her favorite things about him enhanced and more appealing than ever.

Yet, she was sure she couldn't, shouldn't trust what she was feeling right now, as it could be just a by-product of the upheaval in her life. Coming to terms with the losses she'd sustained didn't automatically inure her to the pain, and the fear of losing more. Maybe Kiah represented stability, and she was grasping at the safest straw she had, because she'd been adrift so long?

Thinking about it that way made her a little sad, and she sighed.

"Everything okay over there?"

Kiah's question shook her out of her reverie, making her realize the conversation between him and Charm seemed to have stopped. She half turned to send him a smile.

"Fine, just wondering what they'll have me doing at the hospital on Monday. What time do we leave to get there?"

His eyebrows quirked up slightly as he threw her a quick glance. "I'm on call tomorrow night, but if there's no emergency and I'm not called in, I'll leave home at about seven, drop Charm off to school and head into the hospital then."

"And what happens if you're called in and already at the hospital?"

"There's a taxi driver who'll come for Charm. He can drop you off then, too, or come back for you afterward, if you don't want to be up so early."

"My friends at school like it when Uncle Kiah drops me off." Charm's comment, dripping with scorn, came from the back seat. "They think he's cute."

"I think he's cute, too," Mina couldn't help saying, casting Kiah a mischievous grin. "Don't you?"

"He's all right," Charm said grudgingly. "But my friends get all silly over him and that's gross. He's so *old*."

They'd turned off the coast road and were going up into the hills. Kiah took his foot off the accelerator.

"Okay, that's it," he said, shaking a fist in the air. "I'm letting you out here. You can walk home, missy."

"How far are we from Salty's? I'll just stay there," came the irrepressible reply, and Mina couldn't hold back her laughter.

As it turned out, it wasn't that far from the roadside shack. As they pulled up, Mina was surprised at the number of cars filling the small parking area and overflowing onto the road.

"Ah, the parking gods are with me today," Kiah said, when a car backed out of the lot just as they pulled up.

After he'd slotted his car into the space, they all got out, and Charm ran off right away to join the line, leaving them to follow at a slower pace. Kiah slung his arm over her shoulders, the way he often did, but today it felt heavier, his muscles more solid, and a shiver of awareness traveled down Mina's spine.

"So you think I'm cute, huh?"

"Don't be fishing for compliments, Hezekiah." She tried to channel Miss Pearl, making her voice stern, but he just chuckled, tightening his grip on her.

"I don't find it complimentary that a bunch of twelve-year-olds are standing around ogling me. It fills me with self-doubt. Are they the only ones who think I'm cute? Is that why I can't get a date?"

They'd paused under a shady tree, where they could see Charm's slow progress toward the head of the line without having to join her in the hot sun.

"You can't get a date because you're not looking for one," Mina reminded him.

"True," he replied easily. "But speaking of dates, Henkel looked like he was putting some serious moves on you last night. Did he ask you out?"

She glanced up at him. There was something almost too casual about the way he'd spoken, but with his dark glasses firmly in place, she couldn't read the expression in his eyes.

"No offence to your friend, but I think he'd make moves on any woman who crossed his path. I didn't take him seriously at all."

"He's not a bad guy, and usually is more talk than action, but I got the impression he really was into you."

"I'm not interested in anything like that, right now."

"Like what? Going out? Having a little fun?"

She found herself tucking her left arm up under her right, where it was safely out of sight.

"Not interested in being gawked at, like a freak."

Kiah dropped his arm and, putting his hands on her shoulders, turned her to face him. His expression was solemn, with a hint of temper tightening his lips.

"First off, you're not a freak, by any means. You're the same gorgeous, wonderful woman you've always been. And secondly, I was not suggesting that you put yourself in a position where Henkel would be *gawking* at you."

Even with him saying those lovely things about her, the tone of his delivery sparked her temper in return, and she gave him a narrow-eyed glare.

"What kind of position is that?"

He put his face down close to hers, so his breath brushed across her skin when he spoke.

"Like sleeping with him."

Although that was what she was expecting, Mina couldn't find an answer, her brain short-circuiting. It was on the tip of her tongue to say, *I don't want to sleep with anyone, except you.* Thankfully, her tongue had cleaved to the roof of her mouth, making uttering even a single word impossible.

Heat trickled out from her core, and her knees suddenly weakened.

What would it be like to make love with Kiah, feel those strong, wonderful hands on her skin?

Just the thought had a sheen of perspiration breaking out on her brow.

Mortified at the turn her thoughts had taken, she ducked out from under his hands and away from his too-intent stare.

"Just because I'm recently divorced doesn't mean I'm desperate," she said, as much to herself as to Kiah. "You don't have to worry that I'll *get on bad* while I'm here and embarrass you."

And before he could reply, she changed the subject, asking about the hospital protocols, and if he had any idea of what she'd be facing.

Already she knew she was really just a figurehead, a paper tiger being used to make the hospital look good to the Clinicians' Union, but that no longer stung the way it had before. She was trying to see it as a foot in the door, and a way to figure out what else might be possible for her in the future.

"I was told you'll have a staff of administrators to help you get the systems in place," Kiah said. He knew she hadn't really paid much attention to the reams of information they'd sent her in Canada, and he hadn't pushed her to look at it, seeming just content to get her agreement to come back to the island with him. "But I also think you'll be asked to see patients, like you did for John. Hopefully, that works for you."

"That should be fine," was what she said out

loud, but inside she was thinking it would be doubtful she'd be seeing many patients. After all, the scuba accident was an anomaly, and surely the hospital had other competent orthopedists?

"Charm's almost at the counter," Kiah said, touching her arm. "Let's go."

Once they got their food, they found a spot at one of the picnic tables set up among the trees, and tucked in to their chicken, roasted yam, and, of course, roasted corn.

"I remember having this when I came on vacation from med school that year, and it tastes just as good now," Mina remarked, between licking delicious barbecue sauce off her fingers.

"Clearly we're going to need more napkins," Kiah said and got up to head back to the counter for some.

As he passed another table, one of the men sitting there called out to him, and Kiah stopped to chat.

Charm sighed. "Everywhere we go, people know him."

"Well, St. Eustace isn't very big, and he's well known because of his work, so it isn't too surprising."

Charm didn't seem terribly impressed with that explanation and shrugged. "Yeah, but it would be nice to have him all to myself sometimes."

Ouch. Was that aimed at Mina, too? It seemed to be, when Charm went on to ask, "Auntie, are you going to live with us forever?"

Hoping to reassure the young girl, Mina shook her head.

"No, I won't be," she said, giving Charm a smile. "I'll probably be with you all for a month and then I'll go back to Toronto."

Charm gave her one of those level looks that seemed too adult for such a young face.

"I think you should just stay with us," she said, surprising Mina no end. "Everyone's happier when you're around. Especially Uncle."

Not knowing what to say to that, Mina took a bite of roasted yam, hoping Charm would find something else to talk about. But when the next conversational salvo came, Mina realized the first one would probably have been a better bet.

"Auntie, do you think I'm too young to have a boyfriend?"

Good Lord! Why was she the recipient of this particular question? Then she realized Miss Pearl would probably go ballistic if Charm brought it up with her, and Kiah…well, Kiah, out of sheer terror, would probably tell her to stop her foolishness.

"Do you want a boyfriend?" she asked, trying to buy a little time to gather her thoughts.

Charm twisted her lips to one side, looking so

much like Kiah it was almost comical. "I don't know. Some of my friends keep saying they have boyfriends, but I think most boys are gross and silly."

"Well, just because your friends say they have boyfriends doesn't mean you have to, as well, if you don't want one. Besides, boys don't grow a brain until they're a lot older than you all are now, so you'll probably keep thinking they're gross and silly for a few years yet. Give it a bit more time before you get into the whole boyfriend thing, is my advice."

Charm giggled. "You're joking, about boys not having any brains, right?"

Mina nodded, chuckling, too. "That's what my mother always said, and it made sense to me. I have a brother, and I thought he was a mess for a long time. It wasn't until he was in his twenties that I thought he was actually growing up."

Charm's eyes widened. "Will I have to wait that long before I start liking boys?"

Mina shook her head, smiling, suddenly happy, and proud to have been chosen for this girls' chat.

"No. It'll probably happen sooner than that."

"Oh, *whew*," was the response. "I don't want to be that old before I start dating."

"Wait, what's this about dating?"

Neither of them had noticed Kiah coming

back, and both looked up at him as he stood beside the table. The look of horror on his face made Mina want to laugh, and she couldn't resist giving him a little smirk.

With a shrug, Charm turned back to her roasted corn and said, "Nothing, Uncle. Auntie and I were just talking, and she said boys don't grow a brain until they're older. When did yours grow?"

The dirty look she got from Kiah made holding back her laughter impossible. And it got worse when he replied, "I'm not sure I ever grew one. Or if I did, sometimes I think I've lost it all over again."

Even still laughing, as she watched him slide onto the bench and felt another wave of desire rush through her body, Mina understood exactly what he meant.

CHAPTER NINE

ALTHOUGH HEARTENED BY what he saw as Mina's improved outlook on life, Kiah couldn't help worrying about how she'd fit in at the hospital. Not that she was difficult, or hard to work with, but small Port Michael Public Hospital was a far cry from the huge Toronto South.

Which was why he didn't interrupt when he heard Miss Pearl telling Mina, "It's going to be different from what you're used to, because all our doctors play as many roles as necessary. You're here in an advisory capacity as an orthopedic surgeon and trained instructor, but that doesn't mean you can't help out in other situations."

Mina had just nodded and murmured her agreement, but Kiah had seen the skepticism in her expression, and knew she was probably wondering what that entailed.

And if she could be of help with only one hand.

By the end of her first week, though, Kiah felt more relaxed about the way things were going.

"It really is different," she told him as they were driving home together. "A lot more paperwork than I'm used to, and a slower pace, until there's an emergency. And they'll call me in to consult as soon as there's even a hint that I might be useful. I oversaw a student nurse wrapping a sprained ankle today."

"Not something you'd usually be bothered about, is it?"

"Nope. But I kind of like it. It's like going back to the beginning. Getting a reset."

"Like residency all over again, huh?"

That made her chuckle. "But at least I get lots of sleep this time around."

The household, too, settled into a routine that Kiah found all too easy to appreciate. Leaving home in the morning with Mina and Charm, and Miss Pearl on the days she was going to the hospital early, too, made him happy. It felt way too much like the way family life should, and he had to keep reminding himself it was only temporary.

And he couldn't help noticing how Charm gravitated to Mina, asking her opinion or getting her to help with homework. At first he worried that Miss Pearl would be upset, or think her role was being usurped. But the old woman didn't say anything, and Kiah often saw her smiling over at the pair, as though happy to see them together.

Then he worried about how Charm would react when Mina left.

She'd lost so much in her young life already. Would Mina's return to Canada distress her?

He already felt as though it would break his heart to see Mina go, and didn't want his niece going through the same thing.

But it was too late to wonder if he'd done the wrong thing by inviting Mina to St. Eustace. She was here, and he'd just have to live with the fallout of his decision.

To add to his concerns, there was a difference in the dynamic between him and Mina, and he was at a loss to pinpoint it, or figure out why. All he knew was that although they talked and laughed and teased as usual, he sensed a reticence about her, as though she was withholding something from him.

Part of him wanted to find out what was going on in her head, but his ego wouldn't let him ask. For most of their relationship, he'd prided himself on being able to read her every mood, and it irked him when he couldn't.

Just as the surging desire he felt for her shocked and annoyed him, although perhaps it shouldn't. If he'd had his way, she'd have been his first girlfriend, but that definitely hadn't been in the cards for them. For all these years, that young boy's crush had been pushed to the furthest recesses of his mind, never to be thought about.

Having her around all the time now, though, brought all the old awareness and emotions swirling to the surface.

He caught himself watching her when she was oblivious, noticing again the graceful, bouncy way she walked, hips and hair swinging; the way light and shadows played across her face. The sweet curve of her lips when she smiled, the siren's call of her laughter.

But he couldn't avoid also hearing his mother's voice in the back of his head.

"Hezekiah Langdon, don't you dare touch that little girl, or I swear on your father's grave I'll beat you within an inch of your life and send you back to your granny. You don't deserve someone like that."

It didn't matter that she'd said it twenty years ago, or that the threat shouldn't mean anything to him now. Back then it had been the worst punishment she could come up with, and she knew it. By then he'd decided he wanted to study medicine, and if he was exiled back to St. Eustace, that probably wouldn't be possible.

He'd also come to rely on Mina and her family to keep him sane and help him learn how to survive, and thrive, in Canada. They'd opened their home to him, let him know he was always welcome. He'd gotten Mina to admit she'd told them about the abuse he suffered at home and, for a while, he'd felt as though Mr. and Mrs. Haraldson were only kind to him out of pity. Eventually, though, he'd realized they treated him like one of their own kids and had grown to depend on their emotional support. There was no way he was risking losing that because he fooled around with their daughter.

So, although Mina was the only girl he'd really wanted back then, he'd decided their friendship and his future were more important, and had put thoughts of being with her aside.

And of course, there was Warren the Worm, who'd swooped in when Mina was just barely sixteen, and never left.

He's gone now.

No. He couldn't afford to think that way. Nothing had changed, really. He still couldn't afford to lose her friendship, albeit for much different reasons. He also couldn't offer her anything she couldn't find, get, or have on her own.

If it were anyone else, he'd be sending out feelers, trying to see if they were interested in an affair. But this wasn't some random woman he could sleep with and then walk away from without it leaving scars.

In fact, even having these thoughts was shocking. He'd invited her to the island to help break her out of her funk, not to complicate her life, or his, further.

Putting it to himself that way helped, if only minimally.

Partway through her second week at the hospital, she sought him out for some advice.

"I got a call from a coach in Trinidad, asking me to examine one of his players—a youngster named Yanique Smith—who's been having issues with his shoulder. I told him I'd call him back, but I wanted to check to see what the protocol is."

Kiah whistled. "Smith plays on the Trinidadian under-sixteen national cricket team and is being touted as the next Andy Roberts."

Mina's blank stare made him chuckle. Canada may also be an ex-British colony, but they didn't share the rest of the Commonwealth's obsession with cricket, as her befuddlement made clear. "Who on earth is Andy Roberts?"

"He was a top fast bowler for the West Indies, and this young man is said to be on his way to being as good, if not better."

"Be that as it may, I don't know how to handle this. I don't even know how his coach heard I was here, or whether it's against hospital protocol to have patients fly in from outside for private consultations. Besides, I don't want to step on any toes. I'm sure they have perfectly capable orthopedic specialists in Trinidad."

"I'm guessing it's one of two things," Kiah said, turning her toward the executive offices. "Either word has got out that you're here, through the Clinicians' Union, and the coach wants to have Smith looked at by the best doctor he can, or he doesn't want it to get out that Smith is injured. Taking him out of Trinidad to get treatment could make it less likely that the public finds out."

"Okay," she said slowly. "So what do I do?"

"Check with Dr. Hamilton. As the hospital director, he can advise you better than I can."

It was the first of several calls from other islands, and even South America, with patients wanting to be seen by Mina—some for diagnosis, others for second opinions.

Passing Dr. Hamilton a couple days later in the hallway, Kiah found his arm grasped, and himself the recipient of a huge grin.

"Kiah, this idea of yours to have Dr. Haraldson come here was brilliant. She's already increasing our profile, and revenue." The older gentleman gave Kiah's arm a shake and continued, "Please start working on her to get her to stay on permanently. At this rate, we would be devastated to lose her after only a short time."

Kiah could only smile weakly and say he

would, although he had no intention of doing any such thing. He couldn't even think about her staying permanently with any equanimity, much less broach the topic with her.

Worse, he was starting to think she was staying too long as it was.

No matter how he argued with himself that physical attraction had no place in their relationship, he couldn't stop wanting her.

How was he going to resist her much longer?

Mina found herself far busier than she'd ever expected.

She'd thought they'd stick her in an office and mire her down with paperwork, only trotting her out when they needed to show her off to the Clinicians' Union, but it wasn't like that at all.

Instead, she found herself doing all kinds of things she hadn't done in years, not all of which included anything to do with the musculoskeletal system. And it was always a joy when she was called on to work with Kiah.

Somewhere along the line, she'd forgotten just how good his technique and bedside manner were. Watching him put patients at ease or comforting someone in pain just made her heart ache a little. Yet, hadn't she been the recipient of his tender care all these years? Funny how she'd taken it all for granted.

Trying to put a little distance between them hurt, but seemed completely necessary. Her longing for him, which she'd tried repeatedly to put into perspective and set aside, wasn't abating. Achieving that distance was, however, more difficult than ever, since they were both working and living together.

That was, until a slew of requests for consultations came into the hospital, and it was rare she and Kiah actually shared patients.

"It's not surprising, Dr. Haraldson," Dr. Hamilton told her. "Your reputation is wonderful, and, even though you no longer operate, having you diagnose and suggest treatment options is a huge boon for our patients. And the hospital."

He'd asked her to come to his office, and now he gave her a winning smile. "As it is, I'll like to offer for you the opportunity to join the staff permanently at full salary. We're offering a two-year contract, with the option to extend whenever you want."

Stunned, she just stared at him for a moment, trying to think it through. It was completely unexpected. Hell, she'd been at the hospital less than the month she'd initially thought she'd be.

Getting her thoughts together, she smiled as best she could back at him. "Thank you, but let me give it some thought before I say anything. I really wasn't expecting this, at all."

Even though he looked a little crestfallen, Dr. Hamilton agreed, but asked that she get back to him within the next couple of weeks, and she agreed she would.

Why she kept that information to herself and didn't discuss it with Kiah, she wasn't sure. Maybe because she wasn't sure how he'd respond. Or perhaps she just wanted to make that decision on her own.

After all, she'd come here because he'd suggested it, and she'd been at too low an ebb to make a plan for herself. It was about time she got back to organizing and running her own life again.

Deciding not to do anything about her physical attraction toward Kiah wasn't an easy choice, but one she thought best. The worst-case scenario, which was him telling her she was being ridiculous, and then not wanting to be around her out of disgust or embarrassment, wasn't viable, in her estimation.

The stress of it all was wearying, though, and of course Kiah noticed.

"You okay?" he asked quietly one night while they were sitting on the veranda, and she'd fallen silent, caught up in the questions circling in her mind.

"Sure." She infused as much jocularity into her voice as she could, but he wasn't fooled.

"Don't lie to me, Mina. I know you too well. You've been a little off for the last few days. Are you in pain?"

He was referring to her arm, and she knew that, so replied, "No, my arm is fine."

"So what is it? Are you bored?"

That brought a little huff of laughter. "Are you kidding? I've been running up and down the hospital, trying to learn all the systems and develop new ones, plus getting called to consult. I've had a rising cricket star with bursitis, a Belizean marine biologist with chronic leg weakness after a fall, and a Grenadian soccer player with a broken coccyx. How on earth could I be bored?"

"I didn't mean at the hospital, Mina. I meant here. It's a far quieter life than you're used to."

Didn't he know she'd been happier since being here than she could remember being before? Couldn't he recognize how having him, and his family, had filled her to overflowing.

With her dreams of motherhood shattered, being on St. Eustace, interacting with Charm, was fulfilling a deep-seated need in her heart. The knowledge that Kiah doubted her ability to fit in with them and be happy was enraging.

She turned to glare at him.

Cognizant of Miss Pearl and Charm just inside, she kept her voice soft but infused it with enough ice to make winter in Toronto seem hot in comparison.

"I'm not two, Kiah. Or even twelve. I don't need to be entertained by you or anyone. And, for your information, everything is fine, so stop bugging me, okay?"

He didn't even give her the satisfaction of getting angry with her in turn; he just sat there, nodding slowly, his far-too-knowing gaze searching her face.

"Sure," he said, as if she'd asked him to take her to the supermarket or something trite like that. "Whatever you say."

"Ugh," she said, ready to let loose another salvo.

"Auntie?" Charm's voice floated out from the living room, forestalling Mina's next spate of words. "Can you take a look at this project I'm doing?"

"Sure. Be right there," she replied, still glowering at Kiah.

"Saved in the nick of time," he murmured, having the nerve to smile as she stood up.

Mina paused just in front of him and said, "Sometimes, Kiah Langdon, I don't like you very much."

"But I'll always love you, sweet girl, so that makes up for it."

"Ugh," she said again, turning away so he

couldn't see she'd teared up as his words struck home, and made her feel even worse.

That night, after she'd gotten ready for bed, the phantom pains, which had plagued her for the first few months after the accident and then abated, returned with a vengeance.

CHAPTER TEN

As was Mina's way, she didn't stay angry for long, and was back to her usual self the day after their argument.

But not really her usual self, in Kiah's estimation. Despite her denials, he knew something was going on with her, but she wasn't confiding in him the way she normally would. It hurt him, but he'd learned his lesson and didn't push. Hopefully, when she was ready, she'd let him in on whatever was bothering her.

"I haven't had a chance to finish putting the training plans together, with all the consultations I've been doing," she said to him and Miss Pearl that evening. "I hope you don't mind if I stay on with you a little longer. Maybe just a couple more weeks?"

"Of course we don't mind," Miss Pearl replied, before Kiah even had a chance to open his mouth. "Stay as long as you like."

"Like forever," Charm said as she came into the room on silent, bare feet.

Miss Pearl narrowed her eyes. "I hope you weren't eavesdropping on big people's conversation, Charmaine."

"No, Granny. I was coming down the hallway and heard you, that's all."

But Kiah thought she looked a little sheepish and decided he should talk to her about it later.

More important, he'd noticed shadows growing under Mina's eyes, and especially with him, she was quieter even than before. Miss Pearl noticed, too, and asked if Kiah knew what was going on, but he had nothing to tell her.

Charm was on half-term holidays, almost wild with excitement about a camping trip she was going on with a group from school the next day. Miss Pearl was going, too, as a chaperone.

"You're going to camp, Miss Pearl?" Mina asked, obviously surprised.

"No, child," was the stout reply. "The youngsters will sleep in tents, and a couple of the mothers will, too, but there's a nice little cottage, with a bed for me to sleep on. I think they only invite me because of my cooking."

"That's not true, Granny." Charm sounded genuinely outraged at the suggestion. "You're a lot of fun, too."

Both Kiah and Mina were off for the day, and when Mina suggested they take Charm to the beach, he jumped at the chance. He knew how much Mina loved the ocean, and she'd resisted going since she'd been on St. Eustace.

It gave him further hope that she truly was on

the mend, notwithstanding whatever was troubling her.

"Will your arm be okay in the sea, Auntie?" Charm asked with a little frown.

"In the hospital we use salt water to clean wounds," Mina replied. "And although that's sterile, not seawater, my arm will be fine. Mind you, I wasn't planning on swimming anyway."

With preteen logic and no hint of discretion, Charm asked, "So what's the use of going to the beach, then?"

"To get some sun?"

That earned her one of Charm's dry-as-dust looks, and Kiah stayed out of it, squelching both the urge to laugh and to suggest they do something else instead.

Mina had to make up her own mind, at her own pace.

When she came back out, dressed for their excursion, she was once more wearing a long-sleeved shirt, but it was light and gauzy, clearly showing the bikini top beneath.

Miss Pearl was fussing that she hadn't known they were going to the beach that day.

"I would have fried up some chicken for you to take."

"Don't worry, Granny," Kiah told her, stopping to give her a kiss as he went by. "We'll grab something on the way."

"Some foolishness, like fast food. It's not good for you, you know."

Probably trying to distract her, Mina asked, "Aren't you coming with us, Miss Pearl?"

That earned her another dry look for the morning.

"Child, my last swimsuit rotted away to nothing about twenty years ago, and I have no intention of replacing it. Kiah, make sure you take an umbrella, and Charm, did you put on sunscreen?"

"Yes, Granny."

Miss Pearl gave Mina the same searching look. "Have you?"

"Yes, ma'am," was the meek reply, and Kiah had to turn away so neither of them saw his grin.

The beach at Rickard's Cove was packed with both locals and tourists, but they found a spot not too far from the water to put down their beach mats and hoist their umbrella. As Mina settled in under the shade, Charm was already shucking her sundress in preparation for running down to the water.

Kiah sat next to Mina, watching as Charm was diverted from her dip by some school friends calling her name. In an instant, she went from eager child to jaded preteen, joining the little gaggle of girls on the sand. The little cadre chatted and giggled, eyeing some boys who were also huddled together a little way away.

Not too long ago, she'd have been nagging him to come into the water with her, or to play with her in the sand.

He sighed. "She's growing up so fast."

"Mmm-hmm," Mina agreed. "I still have a hard time believing she's almost a teenager. Time has flown."

"She's so smart. I keep hoping she'll give up on the idea of going into show business and become a doctor."

Mina laughed softly. "Medicine is a calling, and you know it. Remember some of the people we went to school with, who were studying to be doctors only because their parents wanted them to? They were mostly miserable and lost. You don't want that for Charm."

"No."

But there was a melancholy weight on his heart. Nothing to do with thoughts of Charm's future, which he was sure would be bright, no matter what she decided to do.

As so often happened, Mina seemed able to read his mind.

"Karlene would be so proud of her and of the job you're doing, Kiah."

"I like to think so," he replied. "But I wish she were here to raise Charm herself."

Mina's hand was cool against his shoulder, her fingers squeezing gently.

"I know you do."

When he laid his cheek against her hand, she sighed and squeezed again.

Mina was quiet for a moment, and Kiah turned to watch Charm and her friends. The boys were setting up to play cricket on the grassy stretch between the sand and the parking lot, and the girls were watching them, all giggles and sassy smiles.

Lord, it was too soon for that particular can of worms to be opened, in Kiah's opinion. Just the thought made his stomach curdle. When it came to his niece, he definitely wasn't ready to deal with the boyfriend-girlfriend thing just yet.

Yet, said a little voice in the back of his head, *at that age weren't you secretly pining for the very woman sitting next to you?*

That may be true, but he really didn't want to think about it right now. Not with the sensation of her hand on his shoulder, the gentle sound of her breathing reaching his ear, even over all the ambient noise.

A group of four young women strolled by, and Kiah, still lost in his thoughts, hardly noticed, until Mina sighed and said, "Wouldn't it be nice to be that age again, but with all the knowledge we have now? Before all the failures of life piled up on us, and everything seems so much harder?"

She sounded so pensive he sat up straighter and turned so he could see her face.

"What failures, Mina?"

"Oh, like my marriage, my career, my life." She smiled slightly and lifted one shoulder in an abbreviated shrug. "Stuff like that."

His rush of emotion was visceral, almost too much to handle. Tenderness, anger, worry, all tangled up together and froze his vocal cords for a moment. When he could finally find his voice, he asked, "How can you classify your life as a failure?"

She waved her hand, as though trying to brush his words away, but still replied, "I know I've done some good, professionally, but in my personal life, I've failed. I let my dreams fade away instead of fighting for them, and let Warren dictate what I could and couldn't have. I fell into the trap of trying to be the perfect doctor and the perfect wife and didn't really spend the time to think about where I'd end up."

"What did you want and didn't get?"

He was almost afraid to hear her answer. Somehow already knew what she'd say.

"I wanted a more balanced life, with time to spend doing things other than working and networking. More time outdoors or traveling. And…"

She looked away, out over the ocean, as though no longer willing to face him.

"And what, sweet girl?"

"I wanted a family."

Mina spoke so softly he shouldn't have been able to hear her, but he did anyway, and the words ripped through him. Strange to think it was something they'd never talked about over all the years of exchanging confidences, something she'd never mentioned and he'd never asked.

With hindsight, Kiah realized he'd probably been dreading hearing she was pregnant with Warren's child, hence his reticence.

Was it horrible to be glad it had never happened, even if only because Mina could make a clean break from the worm without the constant tie of being the mother to his children?

But that wasn't what she needed to hear right now, and he knew it.

"You can still have a family, Mina. You're still young."

It shouldn't hurt so much to say it, but his chest literally ached as the words left his mouth.

She shook her head, trying to smile although her lips trembled a little. "It feels as though it *is* too late. I don't know if I ever want to marry again, and I'm still trying to come to terms with getting along without my hand, and figuring out what the future holds, career-wise. By the time I sort those things out..."

He wished he could tell her it would all work out, that he would make it work out for her, but that would be a lie. Instead, he said, "You're getting there, I can see the changes already. Take it one day at a time. See where things go. But if you want a family, I know you'll make it happen. That's always been your biggest strength—your determination, and the drive to get whatever it is you set your mind to."

Her lips quirked. "According to Warren, no man in his right mind would want a washed-up surgeon with a disgusting stump and no prospects."

Kiah couldn't stop the curse that rolled from his lips, and the anger that overtook him too swiftly to be fully contained. Reining it in took every ounce of his control, and it was still vibrating under his skin when he replied.

"I don't want to hear anything that jackass had to say, and you need to put it out of your mind, too. You're the most beautiful human being I know, inside and out. Any man with a lick of sense would grovel at your feet if he thought it would give him a chance with you."

Even me.

Her lips parted, as though she would reply, but

instead, she looked around and said, "I think I want to go for a swim after all. Come with me?"

Surprised by the sudden end to their conversation, and knowing how self-conscious she was about her missing hand, he immediately agreed. And pride, along with another emotion he couldn't—or wouldn't—name overwhelmed him, as he watched her unbutton and take off her blouse, and then walk, head up, back straight, down to the water.

"Auntie!" Charm came loping over, a huge grin on her face. "You're going into the sea?"

"Yep," Mina answered. "You coming?"

"Last one in is a rotten egg," Kiah shouted, running past them, too full of joy at Mina taking this huge step not to let some of it out.

And he roared with laughter at their twin cries of "Not fair!"

Once she'd made up her mind to stop hiding her arm, it felt as though a weight had lifted off her chest.

She'd told herself, over and over, that she was fine.

Healed.

Back to the way she'd been before the accident.

But it had been a lie.

Now she knew she'd never be that person

again. Accepted that reality. Working again had helped to show her how much she still had to offer. And Kiah's words, said in a way that brooked no argument, made her really think about how much she'd allowed Warren's hateful words to affect her self-esteem. With the light of truth and anger in his eyes, Kiah had illuminated the self-serving lies her ex had spewed so as to make what he was doing seem logical.

The confidence Kiah always had in her, his assertion of faith that she'd get her life back on track, meant more to her than he could ever know. He always knew exactly what she needed to bolster her self-confidence, and let her know she could be, and do, whatever she put her mind to.

Revealing herself fully had taken that assurance to another level.

Sure, there were some people who stared, and Charm had no problem telling them her friends had asked about Mina's lack of a hand, and even wondered how she could still be a doctor.

"I told them that you use your head, and your other hand, to make people well again," she said, not even realizing the profundity of her comment. "You don't have to be perfect to do whatever it is you want to, right, Auntie?"

"You got it, kiddo."

Charm's surety in her abilities warmed her

heart, and seeing the pride on Kiah's face made it all the sweeter.

And she couldn't avoid thinking about Kiah's avowal that there was still time, and a chance, to have the family she wanted. He'd sounded so certain she could make it work, if that was what she decided to do.

She wished she could help him get past his own antipathy toward parenthood. From seeing him with Charm, she knew he was already a wonderful father, and although she knew how much he feared being the type of parent his mother was, she knew he never would be.

It wasn't that she felt everyone had the same urge or desire to procreate that she did, but she couldn't help wondering if old fears, rather than logic and true desires, might be the source of his decision.

That night, exhausted from the sun and the soporific effects of the seawater, was the first in many she slept deeply, unaffected by her arm.

But the next day the pains were back, and it took every ounce of concentration she had, to get through the workday without incident.

The missing hand alternatively burned and itched, driving her to distraction.

Part of the problem, she knew, was that her stress levels were through the roof. The physical therapist had warned her that might happen, but she hadn't paid much attention, especially when the pains hadn't come back during her depression.

She still hadn't given Dr. Hamilton an answer, and the timeframe he'd set was running out. And her unerring desire for Kiah had resisted every effort she made to lock it away.

Until she sorted those things out, she'd have to find some other way of handling the pain.

That evening the household was in uproar as Charm whirred around, trying to pack everything, including the kitchen sink, it seemed, to take camping.

"Charmaine, stop." Miss Pearl's sternest voice only moderately slowed the little girl down. "Pick one of those toys to take with you and put the rest back in your room."

By the time Miss Pearl and Charm were being picked up, Mina had a headache to go with the phantom pains, but she kissed them both goodbye, and stood at the gate to wave until the SUV had turned the corner.

"Wow," Kiah said, slinging his arm over her shoulders and turning her back toward the house. "Let's not do that again anytime soon."

Mina chuckled weakly, just wanting to sit down and enjoy some peace and quiet, although she didn't know how much enjoyment she'd get out of anything tonight.

"Charm's just excited to go on her first camping trip," she said, and even she could hear the weariness in her own voice.

Kiah led her over to the sofa and gently pushed at her shoulders, so she sat.

"You want a cup of tea? Something to drink?"

Concern was patent on his face, those dark watchful eyes trying to divine what was happening with her, and, before she could stop them, tears filled her eyes and overflowed onto her cheeks.

Kiah knelt down in front of her to cup her cheeks.

"Sweet girl. Tell me what's wrong. Please. Let me help you, if I can."

That made her laugh through her tears, but there was a hysterical edge to her mirth.

Kiah used his thumbs to rub at her cheeks, then got up and sat on the couch beside her. When he reached out and pulled her onto his lap, she didn't resist, wanting the closeness, even if it wasn't as close as she wanted to get. Burying her face in his neck, she let his warmth seep into her, fill her.

"What is it, Mina?"

"Phantom pains." It came out as a low moan. Somehow being here like this with him made the sensation increase. "It burns and itches."

"Why didn't you tell me before?" The anguish

in his tone was clear. "What can I do to make it better?"

"Get me my hand back?"

She was trying to joke, to lighten the mood, but his arms tightened around her, and his chest shuddered when he inhaled.

"If I could, I would, sweet girl. You must know that?"

It sounded like he was about to cry, too, and she couldn't bear it.

"I'll be okay, Kiah. It'll pass."

"I know an acupuncturist, but I doubt she's still open at this hour. Damn it, Mina, why didn't you say something earlier?"

Even though he sounded angry, it was the caring she heard in his voice.

"I was trying to handle it myself," she said.

His chest rose and fell on a sigh. "You know that as long as I'm around, you never have to face anything alone, don't you?"

"I do." She sighed in turn. "But sometimes I need to do things for myself. I can't lean on you for everything."

He didn't reply, but there was something about his stillness that made her raise her head to search his face. His expression was intent, and somehow the way he was gazing at her made her heart rate pick up, and the ever-present need flower bigger, and hotter, in her core.

"You can, you know," he said quietly. "Any- and everything. No matter how little, or big, or off the wall. I've always got you, sweet girl."

It took everything she had inside not to let her gaze drop to his mouth, not to tell him how much she wanted him to kiss her and make love to her. Something inside her whispered that would make everything right, but she knew better than to trust that voice. Besides, Kiah didn't think of her that way, and the thought of his rejection was too much to bear.

So, instead, she snuggled her face back into his neck, inhaling the warm, sexy scent of him, even as she tried to ignore the desire flowing like liquid fire through her veins. There was no place she'd rather be than in his arms, so she shifted a little closer on his lap, craving additional contact.

Then it sank into her brain what she was feel- ing snugged up against her thigh and, for a brief, glorious moment, she thought his erection was a sign he wanted her, too. Her heart rate soared, and she tightened her grip on his waist. But even as she felt him pull her in a bit more, sanity re- turned.

The right thing to do would be to ignore it, leave it alone, but Mina felt compelled to com- ment anyway. After all, they'd been calling each other out over stupid or embarrassing stuff for years. Why buck the trend now? Besides, laughing about it hopefully would get her back on an even keel.

"You really have been going through a drought, haven't you?" she murmured, bumping his crotch gently with her thigh, so there was no mistaking her meaning.

She expected a chuckle, or a witty riposte, not the silence that followed her comment, or the restless movement of his hands on her back, which felt suspiciously like a caress.

Eventually, Kiah inhaled deeply, then replied, "My sexual drought has nothing to do with it, sweet girl. That's all for you."

CHAPTER ELEVEN

HE'D HOPED SHE wouldn't notice or, even if she did, wouldn't comment, but once she had Kiah knew he couldn't let her go on believing it was just an automatic reaction on his part. That if it were anyone else, his body would respond the same way. Not after the conversation they'd had on the beach, when she'd told him the disgusting things her ex had said.

No. Mina needed to know she was still as desirable as she'd ever been.

To him even more so than ever before.

Seeing her every day over these past weeks, in all her various moods—vulnerable and confident, laughing, crying, and everything in between—had been an emotional revelation. For so long he'd pushed his attraction to her down deep, refusing to let it grow beyond the treasured friendship. Distance had made that easier, but now there was, literally, no hiding from the truth.

He wanted her, badly.

Mina hadn't responded verbally to his words, but he could feel her rib cage rising and falling rapidly beneath his hands, and her stillness was, in itself, telling. Kiah could almost hear the wheels turning in her head, and it worried him.

Had he frightened or repulsed her? Was their relationship, so carefully nurtured and vastly important to him, in jeopardy, now that she realized his lust for her?

Then she shook her head, just once, against his neck and said, "I know you don't really mean that."

He snorted, wishing he could find the situation more amusing than he actually did. "I mean every word. I'm not fifteen, and I don't get aroused as though I were. Ask Niesha, and she'll tell you she got no reaction from me, although she tried her level best."

Reaching down, he tipped her chin up so he could meet her gaze.

"You think I was kidding when I told you how beautiful you are? I wasn't. And I could have added the fact you're incredibly sexy. I've always thought so, and having you around has reminded me just how much."

Color tinged her cheeks, and that made him chuckle.

"You're blushing," he said, reaching up to run his index finger over her overheated skin. "I haven't seen that in a while."

"I haven't been called sexy in a while," she retorted. "Actually, in forever."

Kiah kissed his teeth, once more annoyed at the thought of how poorly she'd been treated by her scumbag ex.

"You should know it, though. Don't you notice how men look at you? At the club, the hospital, on the beach yesterday? There's an air about you, Mina—sultry and sassy and sexy, all combined to make you irresistible."

It was her turn to make an incredulous noise. "You've never had a problem resisting me."

"Our friendship has always been too important to gunk up with sex," he said, trying to be honest without giving too much away. "Losing you because we slept together and it didn't end well wasn't a chance I was willing to take."

Her gaze searched his, and although her lips quirked into a ghost of a smile, her eyes were solemn. "Is that what sex does? Gunk things up?"

"It definitely can," he said, his heart thumping, wondering where the conversation would end up leading, although he was trying to stay realistic. "If the people involved let it."

"And if they don't let it?"

His heart stopped for an instant, and then set off galloping again. Already aroused, his body tightened, almost to the point of pain, and his lungs seized, making replying impossible in that moment.

The logical part of his brain was telling him not to take this any further, to walk away before things went sideways, but his body... Oh, his body was screaming for him to see where this would lead.

Trying desperately to take the path of reason, he finally found the wherewithal to say, "It would be risky, Mina. Just agreeing not to let it change things doesn't mean things wouldn't change anyway."

She nodded slowly, never breaking eye contact. "But what we share can never really be broken, can it? Dented, or bent, maybe, but I'll always be your friend, and you'll always be mine. My best friend. I..."

She paused, looked down, and once more his breath caught in his chest at the sheer beauty of her, the fact they were even having this conversation slamming home again.

"You what?"

She looked back up, meeting his gaze again. "I don't have a lot of experience, Kiah. You talked about men being interested in me, but it scares me—the thought of being with someone new. These feelings I have for you, those *don't* frighten me. Somehow, wanting you feels right."

She shrugged, as though not sure she'd found the right words, and although there was no lessening of his desire, his heart sank just a little.

He was to be an experiment, then. A gateway to finding out what it felt like to be with someone other than the worm.

Hearing that should have lessened the desire, but it didn't. Instead, strangely, it added another layer to his need, making it even harder to resist the temptation on offer. Trying to figure out why was impossible with her gleaming eyes on him, her hand cupping the back of his neck, as though to pull his lips down to hers.

"God, Mina. You're making it really hard for me to say no."

"Then don't," she replied, then gave a little grin. "I like that I'm making it hard."

She bumped his erection with her thigh again, and Kiah choked on the chuckle rising in his throat. Trust Mina to make him laugh at a time like this.

"You wretch," he said, his arms tightening around her waist against his best intentions. "You're leading me astray."

Her laughter was soft, sultry. "I'm trying my best, but you're stubborn. It's like leading a mule."

His amusement faded, and he lifted his hand to stroke her cheek. "If we do sleep together tonight, and want to again, it can only be for these couple of days while Granny and Charm are gone."

She was still smiling, enticing him closer, as she nodded. "Yes. The last thing I need is disapproving looks from Miss Pearl, or having to explain to Charm why I'm coming out of your room."

Besides, for her it was just for the experience, not the potentially life-altering event Kiah suspected it would be for him.

His brain tried once more to tell him not to risk it, that making love to Mina wasn't safe, or even sane. But her fingers were moving on his nape, making goose bumps fire down his back. And she shifted on his lap, her scent rising to fill his head, driving out all thought of anything other than her and this once-in-a-lifetime opportunity.

"Are you sure?" he asked, even as his head was dipping, the words coming out when their lips were almost touching.

And she replied by closing that gap, and his brain short-circuited with that first, glorious kiss.

There was no time for contemplation, for further worry about whether what they were doing was right or wrong. All Mina could feel was Kiah's kiss.

The vibration into her lips, as he growled low in his throat.

The movement of mouth on mouth, and the sweep of his tongue, seeking entrance.

She didn't just invite the deepening of the kiss, she demanded it, welcoming it with the kind of ferocity she didn't know herself capable of.

This was no tender seduction. Not on either side.

Instead, it had all the explosive power of a lightning storm. The inexorable flood of a tsunami.

He pulled her closer so she felt the pounding of his heart against her breasts, the thrust of his erection now beneath her thighs. Twining her arms around his neck, she strained against him, ravenous for his touch.

His lips left hers and found her throat. The sound that broke from her was one she'd never heard before: rife with need and delight, a symphony of desire.

"Last chance, Mina. Stop me now if you're not sure."

She tried to laugh, but it stuck in her chest, held there by the immensity of her arousal.

"I want you." She finally got the words out, but they were choppy, born on her labored breathing. "I need you, Kiah."

"Ah, sweet girl. My sweet girl. Come to my bed."

"Yes. Oh, yes."

Now things settled, became almost calm. Not her racing heart or skyrocketing need, but the admission of mutual desire gave them reprieve from the rush of desperation.

He rose and set her gently on her feet, standing for a moment in front of her, his dark eyes mysterious and probing. Then he turned and led her down the corridor, and into his bedroom.

She reached for him, but he held her arms, his gaze traveling along her body, sparking reactions wherever it settled. Her breasts tingled, nipples tightening further into aching points. Goose bumps rose across her belly, and her legs trembled.

Slowly, oh-so slowly he undressed her, his hands skimming her flesh, his breath harsh and growing faster with each piece of clothing that fell away. Under his rapt focus, she blossomed, felt beautiful in a way she'd never experienced before. There was no need for words between them. Not now. Not when he looked at her as though she were the most precious woman in the world.

And she didn't feel self-conscious when she was naked and he was still clothed. Rather, she felt eager, bold and powerful.

It was her turn, then. And she took her time, both from necessity and desire. Unbuttoning his shirt single-handed, sweeping across his chest and then one shoulder at a time to ease it away, unreasonably pleased when he shivered and his eyes drifted closed.

She got his pants undone, too, and reached into his briefs to grip the hard length of him in her hand, making him groan and, this time, shudder.

"You'll have to help me with the rest," she whispered, not letting go or ceasing the motion of her hand, fascinated by the feel of him, his obvious pleasure.

He grasped her wrist, and she looked up, only to be snared by the heat in his eyes.

"You need to stop, Mina. You're making me crazy."

"I want to."

"You're bad. But I want to return the favor."

He tugged her in close, kissed her until her head swam and her legs were like jelly. How they ended up on the bed, she wasn't sure; she only knew he was touching and kissing her in ways that blew her mind and sent her body soaring.

Making love with Kiah was everything she'd imagined it would be, and so much more.

More intense.

More arousing.

More satisfying.

He set her aflame, then made that fire into an inferno only he could douse.

She found herself arching, pleading, opening herself to his fingers and lips in the most wanton, beautiful of ways.

When she lost control, it was with joyous abandon, welcoming the ceding of power to his touch, without even a hint of shame or fear.

Now the desperation was back, and she pulled him close, wrapping her legs around him, urging him to fill her, to take her back to that place of ecstasy.

"Mina, wait," he said. "We need to use protection."

With a little growl, she loosened her grip on him, and said, "Hurry."

She lay there, watching him sheath himself, even that mundane action an aphrodisiac. When he came back to her, she welcomed him, and as he slid into her body, stretching her, she mewled with pleasure.

"I want you," she panted, tightening her strong thighs so he couldn't escape. "I need you, Kiah."

He groaned, gave in, pushing forward to give her his entire length, and she cried out.

"Yes. There. Oh, yes."

He shifted, went even deeper, then began to move, each thrust and retreat causing little spasms deep within her, until they all started running together, and she found herself once more on the edge of completion.

"Mina. Mina. Mina."

It was a chant, a benediction, and her body responded, as though the sound of her name in his hoarse, desire-struck voice was the final touch she needed.

Her orgasm came with the force of a runaway train, barreling through her, causing every muscle and sinew to stiffen, shutting down her nervous system, making lights flash behind her tightly closed eyes.

And hearing, feeling Kiah join her, took the sensations straight to sublime.

CHAPTER TWELVE

KIAH LAY IN the dark, wondering if he was dreaming.

It all felt too good to be reality, and he wished he could, like Mina had, fall asleep, so as to hold on to the perfection.

But although his body was sated, his brain wouldn't shut off, his thoughts confusedly swinging from euphoria to fear, and back again.

They'd made love. Him and Mina. She'd shared her body with him in the most wonderful, meaningful night of his life.

Their kisses, the love they'd made, had been sheer perfection.

He'd been right to worry making love would change their relationship, and use that instinctive knowledge to try to stop it from happening. He already felt a shift inside, the emotional bond he'd always had with Mina transforming in a way he didn't want to contemplate.

It scared him, the way she'd made him feel, the rightness of touching and kissing her, the joy he'd gotten from hearing her cry out in pleasure. The utter ecstasy he'd experienced in her arms.

Down this road lay the type of madness he'd tried so hard to avoid all his life.

The insanity of love.

His mind whirled, bringing up ghosts of the past, as though to emphasize the severity of the danger he was courting.

His father collapsing, dying in front of him.

Mom, losing the only stabilizing force in her life, and morphing from a relatively normal person into something close to a monster, turning on her children, blaming them for everything.

Kiah had had the Haraldsons to run to when things got bad at home. Karlene hadn't been so lucky.

"Those damn people done steal one of my children." He heard his mother's voice, as clear as it had been that night, when he'd tried to take Karlene with him, just to get her away from his mother's poisonous tongue. Remembered her crazed stare as she held on to Karlene, silently daring Kiah to tear her daughter from her arms. "They not getting the other one."

He'd had to turn away from the plea in Karlene's eyes, and make his escape.

Roy, battered and broken in spirit after a bomb had killed four of his friends, tearing through the troop transport he was on. Unable to function, despite his love for his wife and daughter, harangued by his mother-in-law at every turn.

Kiah had seen it firsthand while visiting Canada, and he'd tried to tell Karlene what their mother was doing wasn't healthy.

She'd shrugged. "She's trying to help me out, Kiah. Taking care of Charm when I have to work. I don't listen to her when she's bad-mouthing Roy. He's a good man."

"Tell her not to come over anymore," Kiah had said. "She just upsets Roy, and he doesn't need that right now."

"How can I tell her she can't see her grand-daughter, when she's helped me out all this time?"

And no matter what he said, Karlene made excuses for Mom and, in Kiah's estimation, her devotion to their mother had cost Karlene her life. Cost Roy his, too.

Funny how, until Mina had mentioned it, he hadn't thought about what Charm might think of her father. Kiah had been too busy hating him to even consider talking about him, although they'd had a good relationship in the beginning, and Kiah had thought him perfect for Karlene.

And Roy had loved Charm. Somewhere there were pictures he'd retrieved from Karlene's house after the horrific tragedy. Pictures that showed Roy holding his daughter at various stages of her life. That showed his absolute love and devotion.

How could that love not have stopped him from doing what he did?

Those were the questions that made Kiah afraid.

He'd examined his own character and knew there were situations he absolutely needed to avoid. He was as faithful and caring as his father, who'd put up with his wife's moodiness and meanness without complaint, but he also had his mother's temper. He'd discovered that young, when he'd finally had enough, and had gone toe-to-toe with Mom, unable to stop himself from shouting right back at her. Having to walk away when he realized he was about to completely lose control, fearful of what might happen if he did.

The more you cared about people the easier it was to hurt them, or be hurt in return. He'd had enough of that to last him a lifetime.

He and Mina had crossed a treacherous line tonight, and now he'd have to deal with the fallout. Unfortunately, the only way he'd be able to know what came next would be to see how Mina reacted in the morning.

But he wanted her again.

Desperately.

If this was to be the only night they spent together intimately, he wanted it to be as intense and memorable as possible.

Enough to last him the rest of his life.

So he woke her slowly, bringing her up from sleep with gentle caresses.

She stretched in his arms, her hand finding the back of his neck, pulling him down for a kiss.

If he could die then, in her arms, kissing her sweet mouth, he'd go a happy man.

"Kiah," she said, his name infused with such longing his heart dipped and raced to hear it. "You make me feel so good."

"That's my aim, sweet girl," he replied, touching her softly, trying to retain the memory of her silky flesh, the heat and need of her, in his fingertips.

"You've exceeded your goal."

Then words were unnecessary as their bodies took over, desire rising like flames to lick at their skin, demanding they touch more, kiss harder, wrap around each other, as though never to let go.

Need, sharp and undeniable, brought them back together, Kiah sinking into her, losing himself in the rhythm of love. Tumbling, as though down a mountain, when she cried out, clenching around him, and threw him into orgasm.

Mina awoke with bliss still echoing through her body, and lay still for a moment, savoring it. Beyond the window, birds were chirping and doves were cooing, enhancing her sense of well-being.

A small part of her was still disbelieving, a little shocked at what had happened the night before, but the rest of her practically purred, sated and love-drunk.

Wanting more.

A smile curved her lips, and, even to her, it felt sly.

"Hey, sleepyhead." Kiah's deep voice sent a thrill of desire down her spine. "You're finally awake."

Opening her eyes, she blinked over at him. He was smiling, too, but his gaze was shadowed. Watchful.

Mina's stomach rolled.

"Hey yourself," she replied, hitching herself up on the pillows so they were eye to eye.

"How're you feeling?"

Did he mean her arm, the rest of her body, or emotionally? Mina tried to figure it out but failed. Kiah was holding his own feelings close to his chest. Best to just jump in with both feet, since that had always been their way.

"My arm feels fine, and the rest of my body is humming, it's so happy."

So maybe not both feet, since she hadn't mentioned anything about her head space. She'd held back, waiting to see where he was at, before she said the wrong thing.

His eyes sparked with a hint of the fire she'd seen in them the night before, and her nipples tingled as goose bumps broke out across her shoulders.

Then the light faded, and he rubbed his hand across his chin, his morning stubble rasping beneath his palm.

"I need to know that what happened hasn't changed anything between us," he said, giving her a level, guarded look.

"We agreed it wouldn't."

"I know, but I—"

"You what?"

She wasn't letting Kiah off the hook. Whatever he had going through that head of his needed to be let out. Expressed clearly, so there was no miscommunication.

"Dammit, Mina. You know you mean more to me than anyone outside of my family. I need to know you're okay with what happened last night. That we're okay."

Tilting her head, she took in his expression. There was a hint of anguish in his eyes, and his lips were tight, almost angry. No matter what she felt, she knew he needed her reassurance.

"Kiah, nothing, and no one, could ever change what I feel for you. Last night was amazing.

Magical. I've never been so thoroughly satiated in my life, and I'm glad I found that with you, because I trust you more than anyone."

His expression lightened, and, for the first time that morning, his smile touched his eyes, as well as his lips.

"Okay. Good." His eyelids dipped, and his smile changed, becoming sensual. "It was amazing for me, too…"

She smiled, and although she knew she should just take what she'd already been given, and not get in any deeper, said, "Want to see if it's as good in the cold light of day as it was last night?"

"Oh, yeah," he said, his lips already just a breath away from hers.

And it was even more glorious than it had been before, Mina thought later as she stood under the shower, after Kiah had left to go to work.

Thank goodness she was off that day, because there was a lot she needed to work through, and it would definitely have distracted her from her job.

Why did it feel as though her entire life had led up to last night? That the experience of making love with Kiah was the most perfect moment she'd lived?

He didn't see it the same way, she realized. It seemed that, to him, what had happened was a one-off. Or a three-off in this case. Maybe even a more-off, since Miss Pearl and Charm weren't back until tomorrow, and they had the place to themselves tonight. Apparently, he was okay with letting this new, sexual component of their relationship fall away thereafter.

She wasn't sure she was.

If she'd rediscovered her confidence in St. Eustace, it felt as though her deepest, most sensual and loving self had come to light in Kiah's arms. Giving that up, just as she'd found it, was a nonstarter.

Not that she thought it could continue on indefinitely. Even without him stating it was only for these few glorious days, eventually, and more likely sooner rather than later, she'd be going back to Canada. Why couldn't they enjoy this new aspect of their relationship for as long as they could?

How to convince him of that was another question, but one she vowed to tackle with vigor and focus. She'd need to be gentle with him, give him space to work it all out in his own way, but that didn't mean she had to be passive. It wasn't her style, anyway. Never had been, except for those months when she'd floundered, lost and unable to see a way out of her nightmare.

Kiah had been the only one who'd known

what to do, and if it weren't for him, who knows how she'd have ended up?

That gave her pause as she stepped out of the shower and started drying off.

Was she avoiding all her unresolved feelings and issues, and using Kiah's lovemaking as a way to not face them? He'd warned her that sex muddied the emotional waters, even when both parties knew it wasn't going any further.

Was this sexual adventure with Kiah even healthy?

Maybe, she thought, rubbing the towel over her hair, she needed to sort herself out before deciding whether the change in her relationship with Kiah was advisable and should continue?

But deep in her heart, she already knew: a fundamental change had taken place, whether they liked it or not. All she could do was prepare as best she could, and see where it ultimately led.

Then her already chaotic world was further disarrayed by an email from Toronto South formally offering her a full-time teaching position, as the deputy chief of orthopedics.

She sat back, looking at the screen, her heart racing. It seemed like something of a miracle, the culmination of all her career dreams. While they'd originally asked her to stay on as a lecturer, and she'd refused, the position of deputy chief hadn't come up before.

It couldn't have happened at a worse time.

Yet, the choices she faced career-wise seemed nowhere as important as deciding what to do about her feelings for Kiah.

She still hadn't told him about the job offer from Dr. Hamilton, and didn't really plan to tell him about the Toronto offer, either, until she figured out what she wanted to do. Hopefully, the director would be discreet and not spread the word about wanting her to stay.

Part of her rebelled at the thought of leaving St. Eustace; yet, she also had to be practical. Letting her emotions over the change in her relationship with Kiah muddle her thinking wouldn't help her make good decisions.

She spent most of the day going over the tutorial plans she was working on for the hospital, trying to lose herself in work rather than let her mind obsess over the night before. Yet, more than once she found herself staring off into space, smiling, her body tingling at the memories bombarding her.

By the time Kiah got home, she was glad to set her laptop aside, as she looked up to smile at him. His gaze seemed watchful, making her wonder what he was expecting. So she went out of her way to sound casual, almost breezy, as she greeted him.

"Hey," she said. "Long day, huh?"

"Emergency cesarean," he replied, flopping down beside her. "Her OB was on the other side of the island, and couldn't make it back in time to operate. Mom and baby doing well. Father's a blithering mess, though. It's their first."

Mina chuckled. "So many of them are, when delivery time comes. I don't think the fact they're about to be a father truly sinks in until they actually see the baby."

Kiah smiled, resting his head back on the couch and closing his eyes. "And I don't think any of them have a clue what to expect during the actual birth. Intellectually, they have an idea, but the reality still comes as a shock."

There, that was normal, she thought, except for having to battle the urge to grab him, kiss him, take him back to bed. He didn't want that new twist in their relationship to become a regular part of it, so she had to honor his wishes.

Let him make the first move, if he wanted to.

"Miss Pearl left food in the fridge, but I wasn't sure what you'd want. It looks as though she thought we'd be inviting an entire army over while she was gone."

He chuckled, rolling his head to look at her. "That's how it always is, when she leaves even for a couple of days. And when she comes back, she'll want to know why it looks as though nothing was eaten."

"Well," Mina said, stretching, and swinging her feet down to the ground. "In that case I guess I should go and pull something out so she doesn't get mad at us."

"Mmm-hmm," Kiah agreed, even as he was reaching to pull her onto his lap. "Don't want Granny vexed." With a hand on her nape, he tugged her unresisting form close. "She's scary when she's vexed."

"That she is," Mina agreed against his lips, her heart singing, her pulse going haywire.

It wouldn't last forever, she knew, but she'd take whatever he wanted to give.

CHAPTER THIRTEEN

CHARM AND MISS PEARL came back the following day, both exhausted, and with the older lady limping.

"It's just a sprain," she said, when Kiah asked her what had happened.

"We were going down to the river this morning, and Granny slipped," Charm said. "She scratched her hand, too," she added.

"Let me take a look, Miss Pearl." Mina tried to guide the older woman to a chair, gently insistent when it looked like her patient was going to balk. "It won't take a moment."

While she grumbled, Miss Pearl allowed Mina to remove the bandage she'd wrapped around her ankle, so Mina could see the affected joint. Kiah went and retrieved the first aid kit, and, on his return, took a look at his grandmother's hand.

After a thorough examination of the ankle, Mina looked up at the older woman.

"There's a fair amount of bruising and swelling, so you know I'm going to prescribe the RICE treatment, don't you?"

Miss Pearl looked as though she wanted to argue, but Kiah looked up from dressing the cut on her hand to say, "Listen to Mina, Granny, and don't be difficult."

"RICE? What's the RICE treatment?" Charm asked. She'd been leaning over Mina's shoulder, watching what was going on.

"It stands for rest, ice, compression and elevation. Granny needs to stay off her foot for a couple of days, put ice on her ankle and keep it wrapped up. And she should keep her foot elevated, too."

Charm straightened and gave her great-grandmother a long look. "Okay, Granny, you're under chair arrest for the next couple of days, and Sheriff Charm is going to keep an eye on you, so make sure you behave."

Miss Pearl scowled, but no one paid her ill temper any mind, as they all pitched in to make her comfortable.

Once she was settled, with her leg up on a low table and ice pack in place, Kiah said, "Charm, go have a shower, while I get dinner heated up."

"Okay," she replied around a huge yawn. "But somebody's going to have to help me comb out and plait my hair when I'm finished."

"I can help with the combing," Mina said. "But not the plaiting."

"It's my ankle that's hurt," Miss Pearl interjected, sounding put out. "I'll plait it for you when you're ready."

When Charm had gone to shower and Kiah was in the kitchen, Mina fiddled with the remote, trying to find the older woman something to watch on TV.

"Leave that, Mina," Miss Pearl said, the timber of her voice commanding. "I want to ask you something."

"Okay," she said, giving the other woman her undivided attention.

"One of the mothers on the trip is a nurse at the hospital, and she says there's talk that Dr. Hamilton has offered to bring you on staff."

"I heard the same thing."

Kiah's voice was unruffled, and unexpected, since she hadn't heard him enter the room. When she glanced at him, his expression was neutral, but his gaze was watchful.

She felt put on the spot, especially when looking from one to the other she encountered equally questioning gazes.

"It's true," she said, trying not to sound defensive. Then she held up her hand. "But before you start cross-questioning me as to why I didn't mention it, I wanted to think the offer through, before either giving him an answer or telling you both about it. And I also got an email, just yesterday, offering me a position at Toronto South. So I have to take that into consideration, too."

There was a clatter, as Kiah dropped something and it fell to the floor. When Mina finally looked his way, it was no use, since he was bending down to pick the utensil up off the floor, and she couldn't see his face.

"So have you made a decision?" That came from Miss Pearl, while Kiah went back to laying out the cutlery on the dining table.

Mina took a deep breath and kept her gaze fixed on the older woman. She didn't know how Kiah would react to what she was going to say next, and wasn't at all sure she wanted to see.

"I haven't. I spoke to Dr. Hamilton today, asking for more time to decide."

"Well, I hope you make the right choice," the old lady said, more than a touch of asperity in her tone. "I'm not surprised at either of those offers, but I know which one I think is the best fit for you."

"Well, they both came as a surprise to me," Mina confessed. "I wasn't sure I'd even be able to continue practicing medicine, despite all the encouragement I was given after the accident. And I have to say, it's nice to have options again."

Even if both those options left her in an untenable situation.

"We'll have to prepare Charmaine, in any event," Miss Pearl said. "If you decide to go back to Canada right away, she'll be sorely disappointed."

That caused a hard pang of guilt and pain, but Mina acknowledged the truth of the statement. Charm had stolen a big piece of her heart.

"But—"

"Leave it now, Granny."

Kiah's tone brooked no argument, and even though the older woman pressed her lips together, she didn't say anything more. Mina turned in time to see his back disappearing down the corridor to the kitchen, and even just the way he was walking told her he was angry. Miss Pearl looked toward him, too, and then back at Mina.

"You better go talk to him, child. He's upset."

Mina had to squelch the urge to put her fingers in her ears like a child, and insist she didn't want to, but, with a sigh, she stood.

"I guess I should," she said.

Miss Pearl held out her hand for the remote and Mina handed it over, before heading for the kitchen, trying not to drag her feet as she went.

Kiah was at the stove, stirring a pot of what smelled like beef stew, the microwave humming in the corner. He didn't look up when she came in, although she knew, without a doubt, he was aware of her entrance.

"Hey," she said, pausing at the end of the

counter, where she could see his profile. "Are you angry?"

His eyebrows raised fractionally, then fell back into place. "Why would I be angry?"

"Oh, I don't know," she said, unable to keep the sarcasm out of her voice. "Because I didn't tell you about Dr. Hamilton's offer, or the one from Toronto South? Something like that?"

He grunted but didn't say anything, and Mina felt her annoyance level rising. This was Kiah at his uncommunicative best, and it never failed to rile her up. But this time she was determined not to get sucked in.

"I didn't tell you when the offers came in, because I really needed to think it through. To my mind, it didn't make sense getting everyone, especially Charm, wrought up over something I hadn't figured out yet. I've been drifting along, letting things happen to me, rather than taking the initiative. That needs to stop."

Kiah's lips firmed, but he still didn't reply, and Mina sighed.

"Okay, listen," she said, letting some of her irritation bleed into her tone. "Whatever it is you're thinking, let me know when you're ready to share. Because I'm not standing here and letting you make me feel as though I've done something wrong, when I haven't. I'm trying to do the best I can, and if you can't figure that out, tough cookies."

Then she turned and left, hugging her exasperation close, so as not to let any other emotion take over.

Damn Mina.

Kiah tossed the spoon into the pot and just barely missed getting splashed with hot stew.

Of course, he was angry.

Even more so now, after her pseudo explanation.

Was sleeping with him one of those things she'd *drifted* into? From Kiah's perspective, it seemed as though that was something she'd wanted, nearly as much as he had.

And drifting into the job here had done her a world of good, helping to put to rest her worries regarding her abilities since losing her hand.

To make it sound as though all of that was just happenstance riled him up.

Yeah, he could admit the offers she'd received deserved the deepest thought before being accepted or rejected, but it didn't mean she couldn't talk to him about them, warn him. It had been bad enough hearing about Dr. Hamilton's offer through the rumor mill at work, but to also find out she had another offer from Toronto had made his stomach roil.

He pulled out one of the kitchen chairs and lowered himself into it, scrubbing his hands over his face.

Neither her leaving nor staying permanently were things he wanted to contemplate. Both eventualities came with consequences he couldn't even begin to calculate.

It would be better if she left. He'd gotten way too used to having her around as it was, and now that they'd slept together, being near her all the time was doing crazy things to his body.

And his head.

If she went back to Canada, things could go back to normal.

Right?

But he knew he was lying to himself, thinking that they would. She'd made an indelible mark on his entire family. Plus, back home, Mina would have the freedom to date, and sleep with, whomever she wanted, which could lead her to the life she dreamt of.

As her friend, he should be happy with that thought, but it just made him angrier.

Kiah would have probably marched back into the living room and caused a scene if it weren't for the scent of scorching meat.

Jumping up with a curse, he moved the pot off the burner and turned off the fire. Grabbing the spoon made him swear again, and drop the red-hot implement.

He had to get a grip on his anger, if only for Charm's sake. He couldn't let his niece see how upset he was and start asking questions.

Sighing, he went to get a pot holder, and then used it to hold the spoon and gently stir the stew, being careful not to pull any of the burned stuff off the bottom.

The reality was that Mina had already become an integral part of their lives. The sense of rightness of having her here, the joy he got seeing her each morning, riding back home with her in the evening, just seeing her around the place, was unmistakable. Since they'd slept together, that sense of belonging had just grown.

It really was better that she go sooner rather than later.

But he didn't want her to.

He wanted to keep her right where she was.

It was the most selfish impulse ever, and he knew it. Having no intention of initiating any further changes in their relationship and, in fact, being determined to back away from making love with her again, he had no right to make any demands.

If ever it was time to put his money where his mouth was, this was it, and he did his best to stuff all his anger and confusion down, as he dished out the food.

"Charm, come help me carry these in, please," he called.

The youngster came into the kitchen, scuffing her feet, looking so dejected Kiah's heart ached for her. Yet, he knew neither Miss Pearl nor Mina would have said anything to her about what was happening.

"Hey, what's the matter?" he asked, knowing full well what the problem was.

"Nothing."

It was barely more than a mumble, but her eyes glistened with tears.

Putting down the dish in his hand, Kiah pulled out a chair and pointed to it. "Sit."

With obvious reluctance, his niece did as bid.

"Were you listening to the conversation between Granny, Auntie and me?"

"Yes, but it was an accident."

He shook his head. "I don't think it was, Charm. That's a bad habit to have, and you need to stop eavesdropping. If you want to know something, ask, but don't sneak around trying to hear things that don't concern you."

Her lower lip trembled. "I'm sorry. I won't do it anymore, but is Auntie really going back to Canada soon?"

"She might be. But even if she goes back, I'm

sure you can go visit her, if you wanted to." Just the thought of Charm going to Canada made his stomach churn, and added another layer of pain to the whole situation.

"She always said I could, but suppose she changes her mind?"

Kiah chuckled, although the last thing he felt was amusement. "Listen, I've known Auntie Mina since I was the same age you are now, and she never, *ever* says anything she doesn't mean, okay?" Tugging her out of the chair, he hugged her and gave her a kiss on the top of her damp head, adding, "Everything will work out, Charm. Just wait and see."

"Okay," she said.

But although Charm seemed to take heart, Kiah couldn't help wondering if he believed his own optimistic words.

CHAPTER FOURTEEN

DINNER WAS TENSE. Although the adults tried to keep up a facade of normalcy, Charm was unusually quiet and a little surly. So much so that, after she'd helped to clear the table, she declared she was going to go to bed, without anyone reminding her it was time.

Mina found it telling that she wasn't asked to come and tuck Charm in, as she often had been in the past. Instead, it was Kiah who went to make sure she had turned out her light.

When he came back into the living room, he said to Miss Pearl, "Do you think you can manage by yourself for a little?"

"Of course." She sniffed, as though annoyed. "I got back up the hill from the stream after I twisted my ankle, so I'm sure I'll be able to get myself to bed without any problems."

He turned to Mina. "Do you want to go get a drink somewhere?"

"Sure," she said, not bothering to disguise the frost in her voice. "Just let me go change."

She was spoiling for a fight, and she knew it. Whatever he had to say, she was ready to give it all right back to him.

Wasn't he the one, back in Canada, who told her she needed to get on with her life? What right did he have to be upset because she was doing exactly that?

With that in mind, as they were driving toward the Sweet Spot, she said, "If you want to talk about what I told you earlier, I don't think we should do it in public."

He slanted her a glance and said, "Yes, I want to discuss it. So, if that's how you feel, what do you suggest?"

"Let's just go to the beach. We can walk and *discuss*."

But if he thought he was going to berate her for keeping the news to herself, he'd better have a damn good argument, because she was loaded for bear.

The moon was waxing, almost full. The scene at Rickard's Cove, with its backdrop of coconut trees, would have been romantic if Mina wasn't simmering with annoyance.

Kiah waited while she took off her sandals, and then they walked silently together down toward the water. It occurred to her that, before they'd slept together, they'd probably have been holding hands, or Kiah would have put his arm around her shoulders, and the memory made her suddenly sad.

"You think I'm upset because you didn't tell me what was going on, but that isn't true."

She'd been so lost in melancholy reminiscences his voice startled her, but it also brought her back to the moment, and her anger.

"Really?" Injecting skepticism into her tone wasn't difficult at all. "So what is your problem then? Because it sure seems like you're sulking for having been left out of the loop."

"That's not it, Mina." There was a note of frustration in his voice. "Sure, I was annoyed that I had to hear about Hamilton's offer at the hospital, instead of from you, but I have bigger concerns than that."

"Like what?"

"Like Charm's well-being. Yes, I want what's best for you, and I know deciding what that is, is your job. It's just not going to be easy, no matter what you choose. Especially for Charm. She heard us talking earlier, and is upset just at the idea of you leaving."

Of course, he was thinking about the effect on Charm. What had happened between them didn't come into the picture, at all.

Not for him, anyway.

"Kiah, no matter where I am, Charm is always welcome. In fact, I'd love to take her to Canada. I can't think of anything more fun than the thought of showing her around Toronto, or taking her to Niagara Falls."

"That's another thought that fills me with dread," he said, and she could actually hear it in his voice. "Charm in Canada."

"Why? Don't you trust me to take care of her?"

"Of course I do. I wouldn't trust her with anyone else. It's just…"

He stopped and stood facing the water, rubbing his hand across his cheek, the way he always did when upset.

"Just what?" She spoke gently, realizing they'd gotten far from the topic of her job prospects, but not minding. There was something deeper at play here, and she wanted to know what it was.

"I don't want her seeing Mom, and don't know that I can stop it happening, if either of them wants to see the other."

His words rocked her back on her heels, and before she could formulate a reply, he went on.

"Mom's toxic, Mina. You know that. She drove Roy to do what he did, and then had the gall to want to fight me for custody when it turned out Karlene and Roy had made me her guardian. You remember?"

"Of course I do," she said gently, unable to stop herself putting her hand on his arm, out of sympathy, and a shared sense of remembered grief.

It had been one of the worst things she'd experienced. They'd all been shocked and horrified by the tragedy. All except Kiah's mother, who'd told anyone who'd listen she'd known it was going to happen. That Roy was evil, and a wastrel who'd stolen her daughter from her.

Not trusting Warren, even then, to do it properly, Mina had found Kiah a lawyer who'd petitioned the court on his behalf. Somehow, he'd convinced Mrs. Langdon, or her attorney, not to pursue her own claim, and Kiah had gotten full custody.

Outside the courtroom door, Kiah's mother had told him, flat out, she never wanted to have anything more to do with him, within earshot of Charm, Mina and everyone else.

It had been horrid and uncomfortable, and one more blow to him in an already tragic situation.

"I can't let her poison Charm, Mina. Not when she's just getting to the stage that she's wanting to hear about Karlene and Roy. Mom won't have anything good to say about either of them."

He paused, his throat working.

"And she won't have anything good to say about me, either. She never did."

Now she was angry again, but not at him. At

his mother, and the soul-sapping hold she'd always had on Kiah.

Mina tightened her fingers and shook his arm, hard.

"Hezekiah Langdon, you listen to me. You're a wonderful man, an amazing doctor and a fantastic father to Charm. Nothing your mother can do, or say, can change any of that, you hear me?"

He chuckled, but it was edged in pain.

"You have to say that. You're my best friend."

"No," she said honestly. "I don't have to say that, and wouldn't if it weren't true. For instance, if you were a crappy doctor, I'd leave that bit out. Or if you were a mediocre father, I'd be nice enough not to mention it. But I don't recall our friend contract stating anywhere that I had to lie to stroke your ego, so I'm not going to do it."

His laughter was more natural by the time she was finished, just as she'd hoped, but she wasn't prepared for him to turn to her, and say, "So you think I'm a wonderful man, eh?"

Caught in a trap of her own making, all she could do was shake her head and send him a scowl.

"Why're you always fishing for compliments? It's one of your least attractive traits."

Which just made him laugh harder, and when he pulled her in for a hug, it felt so natural to go into his arms, the way she had so many times before.

However, this wasn't old times, and in the new reality she was living, Kiah Langdon wasn't just her friend, but had also been her lover. The man who'd shown her more pleasure than she'd ever dreamed possible.

So being hugged didn't feel safe, or comfy-cozy the way it used to. Instead, her body reacted, heating and softening, her heart rate kicking into high gear, her nipples tightening until they ached.

She wanted him, so very badly, but couldn't have him, and she searched for something to say to distract her from the need weakening her resolve.

"Do you remember the night by the lake, up at my parents' cottage?"

There had been several, but he hummed assent, the sound rumbling into her cheek, as though the shared memory had drifted from her brain into his. "Just before we went off to residency. How could I forget? You asked me to run away with you."

"Yes. I was terrified I wouldn't be able to hack the program. That they'd figure out I was a fraud and kick me out."

"Plus, your mom had that breast cancer scare,

and your grandfather had just been diagnosed with Parkinson's. It was a bad time for you."

"But you talked me down off the ledge. Plus turning me down for the freedom flight."

"I didn't know it was a flight to freedom," he said with a soft chuckle. "All I could picture was your dad and Warren hunting me down like a dog, thinking I'd kidnapped you."

She snorted. "I doubt either of them would have minded much."

He was quiet for a while, and that was when she realized his heart was pounding, too. He shifted his body slightly away from her and, guided by an impulse she couldn't control, she shifted, too, bringing his erection flush against her stomach.

Kiah inhaled, his chest expanding, muscles rippling, and Mina caught back a moan of desire.

How could she want him so much, even knowing it would never lead anywhere? Where was her pride? Her sense of self-preservation?

"Why do I want you the way I do, Mina?" Kiah's voice was quiet, almost contemplative, but rough. "When I close my eyes at night, all I can see is you. When I hear your voice, I remember you crying out my name. It's like you've gotten into my blood, and now I can't get you out."

She was trembling, but made one last-ditch

effort to lighten the mood, to break the spell of moonlight and lust that had settled over them.

"Are you calling me a virus?"

"If you are, I'm afraid it's incurable." Now his voice was anguished, the pain unmistakable to her Kiah-sensitive ears.

It made her realize how much he didn't want to feel that way, how much the change in their relationship hurt him, although she didn't know why. And knowing he was hurting made her hurt, too.

She took a step back, easing out of his arms so as to look up into his beautiful, moonlit and shadowed face, wishing she could see whatever it was in his eyes.

"We don't have to go on with this, Kiah. We can just be friends, no matter how hard that might be. We've come too far to lose what we do have, and we can move forward from this."

When he pulled her back in against his chest and buried his face in the space between her neck and shoulder she thought he was going to acquiesce.

But instead, he murmured, "One more night, Mina. Please. Give me one more night with you."

And it didn't even cross her mind to refuse.

Kissing on the beach, in the moonlight, was enough to drive him to lunacy with the sheer, urgent intimacy of his mouth on hers, the interplay of their tongues.

He knew it wasn't right, that he was flirting with destruction, but Kiah couldn't resist Mina's lure, the need that drove through him each time she spoke, or laughed, or simply breathed.

His hands roamed her body, slipping beneath her shirt to slide across the skin of her back, and he felt the goose bumps rising in their wake when he reversed course. And he shivered at the sensation of her hand on his nape, pulling him closer, and her soft breasts against his chest.

Wanting was like fire in his veins, or lava, making him hard, reducing him to a column of desire, ready and willing to be incinerated by the woman in his arms.

Something about Mina spoke to his soul, called to him, so he raced to her like a sailor to a siren.

She'd joked about being a virus, but at times it felt exactly like that. A virus without treatment or cure, that never left the system but flared up at will.

This, he promised himself, would be the last time he made love with her. If this madness wasn't corralled, contained, it would devour him whole, leaving nothing behind.

"Let's go home," he said, coming up for air. "Before I try to make love to you here."

"We can't, not yet." Her voice was raw, as desire-rough as his own. "Miss Pearl will still be up."

He cursed, dropping his chin down to his chest, her giggles lightening his heart, although they did nothing to tamp down his libido. It was on the tip of his tongue to say he didn't care, but that wasn't strictly true. Granny not only had very traditional views on how men and women should behave, but she also harbored hope he and Mina would get together as a couple.

She hadn't been reticent about saying so to him either, over the years, although surprisingly she hadn't mentioned it recently.

There was no way he was giving her any false hope by letting it be known he and Mina had slept together.

Resting his forehead against Mina's, he said, "The joys of being a thirty-five-year-old man who lives with his grandmother. Why do I feel so much like a teenager right now?"

Her giggles increased, but her hand swept lightly across his cheek.

"Because we're in the kind of predicament teenagers find themselves in all the time. All revved up, and nowhere to go." She kissed the tip of his nose. "Let's go have that drink and re-group. Then we can see how we feel after that."

But he recognized a reprieve when he saw one, and shook his head.

"Let's just go home. This was a bad idea anyway. We both know this isn't healthy." It almost killed him to say it, but he knew it was true. "We can't be together, as a couple, so we probably should stop torturing ourselves this way."

Her amusement fell away, and she tried to search his gaze. With the moon behind him, he hoped she couldn't read the anguish he knew was reflecting in his eyes. Then one corner of her mouth tipped up, and she nodded.

"Okay. Probably a wise plan."

And she bent to pick up her sandals from where they'd dropped onto the sand, and they headed back to the car.

She'd been on the island for only a short time, but it had been enough to tear his life, his heart, apart. The years stretched ahead, threatening his sanity with the knowledge of what his options were—either seeing her all the time but not touching her anymore, or not seeing her at all.

He couldn't decide which would be worse.

CHAPTER FIFTEEN

THE TENSION IN the house hadn't abated the next day, and Mina was glad to be working, although speculative glances at the hospital upped her stress. Knowing the entire staff had heard about the offer from the director and was wondering what she planned to do added to the pressure.

While Mina was in the small staff cafeteria having lunch, there was an all-hands emergency, after a bus carrying dozens of people overturned on one of the country roads. The call went out for all available doctors and nurses to go to the emergency department, stat. Quickly tossing the rest of her sandwich, she took off at a gallop, deciding to take a shortcut through an older part of the building, which would get her to emerge quicker.

Once inside, she was surprised at how quiet it was but then realized they'd probably pulled staff from here, as well. There was only one baby visible in the NICU, with a nurse tending to him or her, and through an open door she glimpsed a mother nursing her child. Obviously, unlike the emergency room, it was a quiet day in the maternity and labor ward.

As she got to the doors leading back outside, they swung open, and a hugely pregnant woman pushed through, almost falling into the corridor. Mina grabbed her, lending her support.

"The baby coming." The woman was panting, holding her belly, and her face was covered in perspiration. "The baby coming."

"Come with me," Mina said, hastily leading her around the corner, toward the labor ward.

But the woman stopped and bent double, moaning.

Obviously, they wouldn't make it to labor without some help.

"Nurse!" Mina called. "Nurse!"

But no help was forthcoming, so, as soon as the mother-to-be seemed able to walk again, Mina hurried her into the first room they came to.

"I'm a doctor," Mina told the woman, trying to be reassuring, although her own heart rate was going wild. It had been years since she'd delivered a baby, and back then she'd had two hands. "Let's get you on the bed and take a look."

"It's coming," the woman moaned, after Mina got her partially undressed and lying down, and went to the end of the bed to examine her.

One peek told Mina the woman knew exactly what she was talking about. Right there, in plain sight, was a little patch of hair.

"Nurse!" Mina bellowed, just as the cell phone in her pocket buzzed. Did she even have time to answer?

A quick glance showed Kiah's name, so she jammed it on speaker and threw it onto a handy chair, on her way to the sink to wash her hand as best she could.

Gloves? What the hell was she going to do about gloves?

"Mina? You there?"

"Yes, but I can't speak for long."

"Did you get the call out for the bus crash?"

"Yes," she shouted in the general direction of the phone, while looking in vain for a sterile towel to dry up. "But I'm delivering a baby."

"You're what?"

"It's coming! I want to push!" yelled her patient.

"Hold on, Mama," Mina said in response, trying not to yell, too, as she grabbed a handful of gloves she couldn't even put on. "Wait until I tell you to push, okay?"

"No. No. I want to push now!"

"Mina, where the hell are you?"

"Maternity!"

Another peek showed it was almost time for the baby to make its appearance, with the mother's cervix almost perfectly dilated. Looking around, Mina spotted a package of disposable bed pads, and, sticking it between her knees, held it with a corner of a glove and tore it open. At least now the baby would have something clean to land on, she thought, as she spread it between the mother's legs.

Having put a glove over it, she laid her stump on the mother's belly, hoping it wouldn't freak her out, and rubbed soothingly, saying, "It's okay, Mama, you're doing real good. Give it a couple more seconds, then you can push all you want, okay?"

"Argh!" was the reply, as the mother arched with the pain of her contractions, but she waited until Mina told her, before she pushed in earnest.

The baby crowned before retreating slightly, and then, as Mina chanted, "Push, push, push," at the mother, the little head emerged.

"Good job, Mama," Mina said. "Now don't push again, until I tell you."

She hadn't been able to put a glove on her hand, so now she used the sterile latex like a pot holder, while turning the shoulders.

Then they were off to the races again, and in a trice, the baby slid out, already crying.

"It's a boy, Mama." Mina felt tears prickle her eyes as she looked down at the wrinkled, slippery little bundle lying on the bed. "You have a baby boy."

"Woo-ee," was the weary reply. "Another one?"

Then, suddenly, there was what seemed like a dozen people rushing into the room, and Mina was able to abdicate her position, although she felt strangely aggrieved about it. She'd delivered the baby, all by herself, but they weren't going to let her cut the cord? It didn't seem right.

But her part in it was over, so, as the obstetrician took her place, she dodged a nurse pushing a cart and turned toward the door.

And there was Kiah, shaking his head, amusement tipping his lips, although his eyes looked solemn, maybe even a little sad.

Haunted.

Why that touched her so deeply, she didn't know, but she stepped close to him, wishing they weren't in the hospital, so she could hug him tight, the way she wanted to.

"Delivering babies now? What's next? Juggling?"

So they were going with the jokes. That suited Mina just fine, and she wrinkled her nose at him.

"Yep," she answered, swinging by him and tossing her gloves into the bin by the door. "With knives."

The triage situation at the hospital lasted most of the day, and Mina found herself back in theater that afternoon, supervising a delicate spinal operation on the driver of the bus.

"In the past, we'd have airlifted him to Port of

Spain, but if you think you can guide Dr. Golding through it here, we'll get him prepped for surgery," Director Hamilton said.

Mina looked at the MRI and CT scans, and talked the operation through with John Golding. Then, reassured the young doctor seemed up to the task, she agreed to oversee the surgery.

Kiah, who'd also been in theater most of the day, came in to observe the operation.

"You missed the best part already," Mina told him, sending John Golding a wink when he glanced up from the endoscope. "John's just about finished, and ready to close."

Since they hadn't been in the operating room more than fifteen minutes at that point, Kiah knew she was just talking smack.

"Why are you even here?" he asked her. "I thought you'd be down in the mat ward again."

Mina sent him a dirty look, before concentrating once more on what was happening on the table. With her guidance, John performed the bilateral thoracic laminotomy, to relieve pressure on the patient's spinal cord, and then spinal fusion on two lumbar vertebrae, all without a hitch.

But, although pleased with the outcome of the surgery, it was the delivery of the baby that stayed with her afterward.

In that moment, when she'd seen the newborn

lying there, she'd realized she really was ready for a family. She'd probably never have a baby of her own, but adoption was definitely an option, in her books.

The decision was bittersweet, since with the realization came the knowledge that the only man she wanted to father her child wasn't interested in doing so. Kiah Langdon, although ideal father material, didn't want children. And even if he did, it was doubtful he'd choose her as the mother anyway. Theirs was a relationship that had taken a turn neither of them expected, but the physically intimate part of it wasn't destined to continue. He'd made that plain despite his obvious desire for her, which, although he'd said it wasn't, actually probably *was* just a by-product of his self-imposed sexual drought.

Yet, however despondent that thought made her feel, Mina knew she'd make it through, no matter what. She'd come to comprehend that, prior to the accident and the end of her marriage, she'd lived a pretty charmed life. There'd been little struggle—if she didn't count medical school—and things had come far too easily for her. Who was she to rail at fate, rather than try to steer her own destiny?

She'd always love Kiah, as a friend and more, but she wasn't going to stop living, just because he didn't love her as a woman.

* * *

As exhausted as he was that evening, Kiah felt restless, and jumpy, too.

When he'd gotten to the door of the maternity ward and seen Mina kneeling at the foot of the bed, looking at the newborn, he'd thought his heart would explode. The expression on her face, one of mingled wonder, joy and elation, was so beautiful he could only stare, enraptured.

Wishing for a moment like that for her.

Wishing he could be the one to share it with her wasn't something he could contemplate and still retain his sanity, so he pushed that particular thought aside.

The barrier he'd built up over the years about fatherhood was too strong to overcome. Seeing his father die, knowing the pain that loss caused both him and Karlene, had made him leery. Recognizing his anger issues, inherited from his mother, had cemented the decision not to have kids of his own. Who knew what kind of parent he'd turn out to be? One who devastated his family by dying early, or one who did it by staying alive and bitter?

Sure, he was nominally Charm's father now, but that in itself only made his choice seem even more sound. There were times when he barely controlled the impulse to holler at her, and he couldn't help thinking sometimes that she was at the age now that he'd been when his father died. She'd already been through so much. He could only pray she would be a little older, on steadier ground, before she had to suffer any more losses.

Like losing Miss Pearl.

After all, she was already in a tailspin over hearing Mina was going back to Canada. Hopefully, she'd weather the parting with a minimum of trauma.

Yes, having a family was something Mina wanted. He could only hope she would one day get it, and he'd have the strength to be happy for her.

Then, as they were all in the living room watching TV, there was a news report about a baby who'd been born weighing a whopping seventeen pounds.

"What is it with babies today?" he muttered, earning a sideways glance from Mina.

"Lawks," Miss Pearl commented. "His poor mother, carrying that much weight around."

"How much did I weigh when I was born?" Charm asked, obviously intrigued.

"Seven pounds, three ounces," Mina said, before Kiah could even think back that far.

"How do you know that, Auntie?"

Mina smiled, and the fondness in the way she looked at Charm was almost his undoing.

"I was there," she said. "It was me who

coached your mom, and I got to cut your umbilical cord, too."

"Really?"

"Really."

Kiah thought that would be the end of the conversation. Even though Mina had warned him that Charm was asking about her mother, he expected her to retreat from any further discussion.

But instead, she asked, "How come?"

"Well, your daddy was in the army, and your mom was alone when you decided you were ready to be born, so I went to the hospital and was there when you popped out."

"Where were you, Uncle Kiah?"

Taking a deep breath, and trying to sound as though talking about it didn't hurt almost more than he could bear, he replied, "I was here, with Granny. You weren't supposed to come for another two weeks, so I didn't get there in time."

"Huh," she said and, thankfully, turned her attention back to the TV.

But later that night, when he went to tuck her into bed, he realized it really had been just the beginning.

"Uncle, do you have any pictures of me with Mommy and Daddy?"

"I do," he said, his heart aching all over again. "Do you want me to find them for you?"

"Yes, please. And…and can you tell me more

about them? Not tonight," she added quickly. "But sometime soon?"

"I can, and I will, sweetheart. Whatever you want to know."

Making his way back to the living room, Kiah felt as though the world, which just a few weeks ago had felt so stable, now wobbled like quicksand under his feet.

"Charm was asking about her parents," he said without preamble, waiting to hear Mina say she'd warned him, and he was amazed when she remained uncharacteristically quiet.

"It's not surprising," Granny said, with a sigh tacked on. "I was wondering when she would."

"Do you remember where we put the pictures, after I came back with her from Canada?"

"Yes. They're in a box on top of my wardrobe. We can get them down tomorrow."

"And I have some I can send back from Canada," Mina added. "I think Charm would get a kick out of some pictures of you in high school and college, Kiah, as well as the ones I have of her parents."

"Lawks," he said, unable to stop himself smiling across at her, even as he shuddered to think how Charm would react to his past fashion sense and hair styles. "You'd do that to me?"

"I sure would. And with pleasure," she added for good measure.

Those were the moments he would miss most when she was gone, he thought. The easy banter. The shared history that came out in stories and jokes.

He was already sure which job she'd take. St. Eustace couldn't hold her, not when compared to the prestige and excitement of the job on offer in Toronto.

He'd miss his best friend, just like he missed having her as his lover, but her going back was for the best. For all of them.

When everyone else had gone to bed, Kiah stretched out on the couch and turned on a documentary, with the volume down low. He knew from past experience he was too keyed up to sleep, and could only hope the murmur of the commentator and the flicking screen would have a soporific effect.

The sound of a door opening down the corridor had him lifting his head, and when he saw Mina come into the room, his heart hammered in reaction.

"Hey," he said. "Everything okay?"

"Fine," she replied as she went by into the kitchen.

After a couple of minutes, she came back with a glass of water in her hand, and paused at the entrance to the hallway back to her room.

"Kiah, can you give me the name of the acupuncturist you mentioned a while back, please?"

He swung his feet down off the couch, instantly concerned.

"The pains have come back?"

She nodded, and he couldn't help remembering how their lovemaking had seemingly stopped them the last time. He knew she wasn't angling for more of the same. That was one choice that had already been settled, although he wished it hadn't. Then he could scoop her up, carry her to his room, and love on her until her missing hand was the last thing on her mind.

But that wasn't feasible, or advisable, so he thought back to all the research he'd done after she'd had the accident, and patted the couch beside him.

"I'll give it to you in the morning," he said. "In the meantime, come here. I want to try something."

She shifted from one foot to the other, as though torn. "I'm just going to take a pain pill and try to get some sleep."

"Come on," he said, giving the cushion another couple of pats. "I read about a technique that's supposed to work kind of like a mirror box. There's no harm in trying it, and you might get some relief. At least enough to fall asleep."

Seemingly still reluctant, she slowly made her

way over and sat beside him on the couch. At his direction, she turned sideways, with her knee up on the cushions, so she was facing him.

"Okay. Now close your eyes and give me your hands."

"You mean hand, don't you?" she asked, cracking an eye open just as he shook his head.

"No. Keep your eyes closed and give me both hands."

Hopefully, she understood what he was trying to achieve, and could trick her brain into thinking he was holding both her hands in his.

As she closed her eyes again, he started a gentle massage on her right hand.

When he felt her fingers tense up, as though she was going to pull her hand away, he asked, "When last did you speak to your parents?"

"Day before yesterday," she replied, and he felt her hand relax with the distraction. "I talk to them at least twice a week."

"How're they doing? Are they still in Florida?"

She chuckled. "It isn't spring in Ontario yet. They're not going back there unless they're sure there'll be no more snow. Dad says he's too old for that nonsense anymore."

"I don't blame him." Kiah hoped his voice was soothing, but having her this close, touching her, even just her hand, had awakened his libido. "That, and the ice storms, make me glad I don't live there anymore."

He adjusted the pressure of his hand, making it a little softer, and she sighed.

Heartened, he continued to speak softly. "And how about Braden? What's he up to?"

"Oh, the usual. He's talking about expanding the acreage, putting in more trees. And I think he's actually getting serious with the woman he's been seeing. He talks about her all the time."

"Have you met her yet?"

"No, I haven't been to BC since they started dating, but I've invited them to come visit here. He's the only one of the family who's never visited St. Eustace."

"That's true," he said, and his voice sounded a little rougher, even to his ears.

He saw her swallow, the movement obvious in her delicate throat, and knew he wasn't the only one who felt the rising erotic tension.

"He…he asks about you all the time." Her voice was breathy, the sound making him want to groan with need. "Says he can't remember when last he saw you."

Kiah couldn't answer. It was all he could do just to keep up the gentle caresses, and not tug her onto his lap, so as to ravish that luscious mouth.

Then there was the sound of a door opening,

and she opened her eyes, catching him staring. He had no doubt the desire in his eyes was unmistakable, as was the current flowing through their one, seemingly innocent, point of contact.

"Hezekiah, is that you?"

They were still staring at each other, their gazes locked, the electric flow holding them bound together, as he answered Miss Pearl.

"Yes, Granny. Me and Mina."

"You two should be in bed."

"Yes, Granny, you're right. We should."

"Go on, then," came the unknowingly fraught reply. "Don't be staying up this late."

As Miss Pearl closed her door again, the tension between them was thick enough to drink, and in the dim glow of the television he saw the rush of color staining Mina's cheeks.

Keeping his voice calm took everything inside. "How does it feel now?"

"Good," she said, the corner of her lips tipping up for an instant, as though she tried to smile but was unable to find the wherewithal. "Thank you."

For a long moment, neither of them moved, and Kiah felt heat billowing out into his veins.

"Go to bed, Mina," he whispered, his gaze dropping to her lips, lingering there for an instant, as he released her hand. "If you don't, I'm going to try to follow Granny's advice."

She nodded, before pushing to her feet. Picking up the glass of water, she took a step away, thankfully before he lost his head completely.

"Night," she said. "And thanks."

"Anytime, sweet girl. Anytime."

Then she was gone, leaving him even more edgy than when she found him, even though he'd thought earlier it couldn't get any worse.

CHAPTER SIXTEEN

Although both Mina and Kiah tried to keep the atmosphere the same as it had been, Charm was still mopey, and Miss Pearl's temper definitely wasn't improved by her enforced immobility.

By day two of the RICE treatment, she was downright testy.

"I don't care what any of you say," she told them all the next evening. "I'm due to run a clinic up at Red Ground tomorrow, and I'm going."

"You should be fit enough," Mina told her cautiously. "But it would be best if you don't stand on your foot all day."

That earned her a sniff and an upturned nose from the older lady.

"I'm supposed to be at Morningside tomorrow, too, Granny, and the hospital is providing me with transport. We could ride together, since I'm passing Red Ground on the way."

He'd mentioned having to go to the smaller hospital to see some patients, and potentially do a couple of elective surgeries so the patients didn't have to traverse the length of the island to have them done. Although Mina was off that day, he hadn't suggested she go with him, and she'd tried not to be hurt by the omission.

After all, it was better to put some distance between them, especially in light of her reaction to his proximity. Just those simple touches last night had fired her libido, leaving her weak-kneed and shaky on her walk back to bed. And once there, she'd tossed and turned, her desire for him keeping her awake half the night. The only good thing was that he'd once more banished the phantom pains, so they hadn't added to her frustration.

"That would be better than driving with Nurse Maxwell," Miss Pearl said. "Her driving is horrible."

"Goes too fast?" Kiah asked.

"No. She doesn't go over twenty miles per hour, and slows down if she sees anything coming toward her. Gives me a headache just thinking about it."

Mina laughed, but the sense of walking on eggshells was hard on her, as was being around Kiah all the time, without being able to touch him. Although it had been normal for them to touch casually, and nothing had been said between them, they both seemed to have come to the conclusion it was better not to, and avoided it altogether.

Then, that night, the strain in the house came

to a head with Miss Pearl barking at Charm, who'd been particularly snippy that evening. Having been ordered to her room by her great-grandmother, the young girl stomped off down the hallway and closed her room door with enough force to almost be called a slam.

Miss Pearl seemed set to shout after her, but Kiah intervened.

"Leave it alone, now, Granny. She's already upset, and if you go after her any more, she'll have a meltdown."

"The child is sulking, Hezekiah. And then she has the nerve to bang the door? In my day, that would earn a good spanking."

"Good thing today is a different day," he replied mildly. "Besides, you haven't been an easy roommate over the last couple of days. Of all of us, you should be willing to cut her some slack."

The elderly lady's lips tightened, but she also looked a little ashamed, and it wasn't too long after that she declared herself tired and went to bed.

"Should I go check on Charm?" Mina asked, wanting to help.

Kiah hesitated for an instant, and then nodded. "Maybe she'll talk to you. I've gotten nothing but grunts and monosyllabic answers from her today."

Was he trying to make her feel guilty?

Whether he was or wasn't didn't really matter, Mina knew, because she felt that way all on her own, without outside prompting.

She'd never thought her choices would have the kind of impact on the others they seemed to have had. Charm in particular was tugging at her heartstrings, even while being a bit of a pain. No amount of reassurance that they would stay in contact, no matter what Mina decided to do, made any difference. Charm seemed to feel Mina was set to desert her, and no one could convince her otherwise.

Mina tapped on her door but received no answer. A slightly harder knock got no response, either, so Mina took a chance and opened the door a crack to peep into the room. What she saw moved her, and made her sigh.

Charm was curled up on her bed, still fully clothed, fast asleep. But there were tear tracks clearly visible on her cheeks, and even in repose her lips were set in an unhappy frown.

Going in, she found the little girl's nightie under her pillow and gently roused her, so that she could change into it.

Still half-asleep, Charm said, "I haven't cleaned my teeth."

"Come on, then," Mina said, getting up and leading her into the bathroom.

When Charm was finished with her ablutions,

it was back to bed, but Mina was a little concerned, as the youngster felt a bit warm to the touch.

"Are you feeling okay, Charm?"

"Yes, Auntie," came the sleepy reply, but she was almost back to sleep before Mina could pull the covers up to her chin.

Bending, Mina kissed the warm, smooth cheek, and slicked her hand over Charms braids.

"Sleep well, baby," she whispered.

When she straightened and turned to the door, it was to see Kiah there, watching.

She put her finger to her lips and he nodded, his tender gaze melting her deep inside.

Walking toward him felt as though it took forever, each step causing the desire that constantly simmered beneath her skin to get hotter, until she tingled with need.

And it was there in his gaze, too, which morphed from gentle to fierce as she neared. When he turned sideways for her to pass him on the way out the door, she could almost feel his arousal coming off him, like static electricity, raising goose bumps on her arm and back. Bringing her nipples to yearning attention.

He took her hand and led her down the corridor past her room, which was next to Charm's, and into his.

They shouldn't be together like this, with

his niece asleep just down the hallway, and his grandmother on the other side of the house, probably still awake. But nothing could stop the explosive desire that swirled and snapped between them, urging them to touch, to taste, to give and to take.

It was an erotic revelation to Mina, made somehow more intense by the necessity for silence, and the knowledge that they had to hurry.

Not that it took Kiah long to make her come the first time. Already he'd learned what aroused her, and how to take her over the edge. He caught her low sound of abject pleasure with his mouth, kissing her until the final shudders eased, and she lay limp in his arms.

Then he kissed her some more, his hands bringing her body back to yearning life, until she was twisting against him, silently, desperately begging for more. The way he caressed her, his hands gentle, adoring, awoke within her a sense of wonder. She became beautiful, because he looked at her as though she were. Became powerful, because of how he reacted to her touch.

Pushing away from him, she tugged at his hand, positioning him on the edge of the bed. When she straddled his thighs to take him deep into her body, it was her turn to muffle the sound of his appreciation with her lips.

It was a wild, ecstatic ride, which culminated

with her biting his shoulder, while he shuddered and whispered words of ecstasy into her neck.

He held her close for several long, sweet moments, as their breathing and heart rates slowly returned to normal. And it felt almost surreal to get up and silently get their clothes back in order, before going back out into the living room.

Mina thanked the heavens when the room was empty. At the last moment she'd had the horrible thought that they'd come out and find Miss Pearl sitting there, waiting for them.

Still without talking, they wandered out onto the back veranda, and Mina sank into her chair with a satisfied sigh. Her legs felt wonderfully wobbly, and the surge of endorphins had relaxed her almost to the point of sleep.

And it was strangely easy to just sit and chat, even laugh a little with him, considering how fraught the last days had been, and how thoroughly they'd broken their agreement. They could go back to staying away from each other the next morning.

At least, that was what Mina told herself.

"I should turn in," he finally said, looking at his watch. "It'll be a long day tomorrow, with everything Morningside wants me to do."

She heard and understood his reluctance but did nothing to waylay him, merely got to her feet and waited for him to do the same, making sure to take leave of him with just a wave. Nothing more.

That way she wouldn't be even more tempted to drag him off to her room and make love to him again.

The next morning Charm said she wasn't feeling well, and went back to bed without eating breakfast. Miss Pearl was unimpressed, even when Mina said she'd thought Charm might have a fever, though the thermometer said her temperature was only very slightly elevated.

"We'll keep her home today, but it's back to school for her tomorrow. Half-term holidays always make it difficult to get children back into the school schedule."

Kiah rolled his eyes but made sure to do it where only Mina could, and his grandmother couldn't, see him. Mina held in her chuckles and somehow kept a straight face.

"I'll keep an eye on her today," she said as they heard the beep of a horn outside, heralding the arrival of their transportation. "I'm sure she'll be okay."

But Charm showed signs of getting worse as the day progressed, complaining of a headache, and with a spike in her temperature that worried Mina. Since it was flu season, even in the tropics, she gave her a dose of acetaminophen and kept an even sharper eye on her than before.

She called Kiah early in the afternoon and left a message asking him to call her back, but before he could, she knew she had to make a decision. Charm was excessively sleepy, and now complaining of joint pain to go along with her blinding headache.

All kinds of horrible thoughts were going through Mina's head, especially with the memory of the not long past camping trip. Encephalitis, meningitis, the dreaded chikungunya—none of them were off the table, in her mind, and she made the decision to take Charm to the hospital.

It was only as she was getting Charm dressed that she realized she also had to figure out how to get her there. Should she call an ambulance? The taxi driver the family used on almost a daily basis?

"Auntie," Charm said with an air of urgency. "I'm going to be sick."

And Mina got her into the bathroom just in time for her to lose what little she'd eaten that day.

That made the decision for Mina.

Without thinking too much about it, she finished helping Charm put on her clothes. Then she fetched a basin from the washroom, and, grabbing the car keys and her handbag on the way out, led the youngster to Kiah's car.

Just as she had finished strapping Charm into the front seat, and placed the basin on her lap in case of need, her phone rang. She answered it as she closed the passenger door and started around the car to the driver's side. The relief swamping her, as she heard Kiah's voice, was visceral.

"Hey, I got your message. What's up?"

"I don't like how Charm looks. She's lethargic, with joint pain and a blinding headache so bad it made her throw up. It may just be flu, but I'm taking her to the hospital."

"Did you call an ambulance, or Mr. Brown?" he asked, referring to the taxi driver.

"No," Mina replied, already sliding into the driver's seat. "I'm driving her myself."

"Jesus, Mina." The stress quotient in his voice rose a number of levels. "How bad is she?"

He knew she hadn't driven since the accident, and wasn't used to the St. Eustace streets, or driving on the left-hand side of the road. Hearing she was worried enough to even attempt it was making him panic.

"I'm sure she'll be all right," she replied, trying to calm him, even though her own anxiety was through the roof. "I'm just playing it safe."

"I'm on my way back, as soon as I find the driver," he said. "And I'll pick up Granny, too."

"Good," she said, glad it was a right-hand drive vehicle, so she could adjust the seat without too much trouble. "I'll call you from the hospital."

Thank goodness the car was automatic, as well, so once she'd got it in gear it was just a matter of steering, and remembering to stay on the proper side of the road.

Charm moaned softly from the seat beside her, wringing Mina's heart.

"What hurts, baby?" she asked as she drove through an intersection perhaps a little faster than was wise.

"My head. The light hurts, even with my eyes closed."

"We're almost at the hospital, okay? We're going to get you all fixed up."

God, she hoped she was wrong, and it was nothing more than a bad case of the flu, but her intuition warned her it was something more serious. Better to be safe, and look like an overly concerned mother, than sorry later on.

When she pulled up outside of emergency, it was to find that Kiah had called ahead to warn them she was bringing Charm in, and there was an orderly and nurse waiting with a wheelchair. As they eased the girl out of the car Charm vomited again, and the nurse and Mina exchanged worried looks.

"Don't leave me, Auntie," Charm said, holding on to Mina's arm.

"I'll be right here, baby, but I have to move the car, in case an ambulance or another emergency comes in. Go with Nurse Schofield and I'll be with you in a minute."

But it wrung her heart to see the fear in Charm's damp eyes, and when she'd found a spot to park and was running back to the building, she had to dash away a few tears of her own.

"Dr. Jonas is in with her," the head nurse told Mina, once she was back inside. "Go on in."

"Dr. Langdon is coming in from Morningside—"

"I know," the nurse said, walking briskly and leading Mina to a cubicle. "He told us what was happening, and said he was giving you the power to make any decisions necessary regarding Charmaine's care until he arrived."

Behind the curtain, she found Neil Jonas examining Charm, with a nurse in attendance.

Mina put her hand on Charm's shoulder and said, "I'm back, baby."

The little hand came up, and Mina grasped Charm's fingers, watching but not interfering, as the examination continued.

After Dr. Jonas was finished, he said, "Charmaine, I'm going to step outside with Dr. Haraldson for a few moments, and then she'll come back in and stay with you, okay?"

Charm's fingers tightened almost painfully. "You're coming back, Auntie?"

"Of course I am." Mina leaned down and kissed Charm's feverish brow. "I won't be gone long."

Seeing Charm like that rattled Mina. She'd become so used to the sassy, irrepressible young woman who seemed older than her years in many respects. Now the child she really was had come to the surface, awakening a deep vein of protective instincts in Mina.

"It could just be a bad case of the flu," Dr. Jonas was saying, and Mina forced herself to concentrate. "But are there additional risk factors I should know about?"

"She went camping over the half-term holidays, up at Justice Peak," Mina said. "It made me worry about insect-borne viruses, perhaps even causing encephalitis, or meningitis."

Neil Jonas nodded, his gaze darting back to the cubicle, before coming to rest on Mina. "I don't want to play around with this. We've had one case of viral encephalitis in the northern side of the island, near to where she was camping, in the last week, so there's a precedent we have to take into consideration."

He took a breath, and Mina's heart dropped,

knowing what he was going to say, even before he said, "I'd like to do a lumbar puncture, to be certain, before I start treating her with drugs she might not actually need."

That was when Mina realized it didn't matter whether you were a doctor, or not. When it was a child you loved, there was no easy way to make a decision that would seem like a no-brainer to the attending physician.

She turned away, tears filling her eyes, and she pinched the bridge of her nose to hold them back. There was the urge to call Kiah, let him decide, but she knew he'd have the very same reaction she was having right now. He also might not be able to bear the thought of Charm going through such a painful, and potentially dangerous, procedure.

Yet, Mina also knew Dr. Jonas suspected, as she herself did, that Charm's illness was serious enough to need medical intervention beyond anti-inflammatory drugs.

Both encephalitis and meningitis could be fatal, or have long-term effects, if not diagnosed and promptly treated. Mina knew she couldn't take the chance with Charm's life and future.

"Okay," she said, turning back to face Dr. Jonas. "Do the spinal tap. Will I be allowed to stay with her while you do it?"

Normally parents were advised not to remain

in the room, but she'd promised to stay with Charm, and she wanted to keep that promise. Besides, she wasn't a parent, and she was a doctor to boot. Surely those things would count for something?

"You can, if you want to." Dr. Jonas gave her a knowing look. "You know better than most what's involved, so if you think you can handle it, then yes."

"Of course I can," she said, with far more confidence than she was actually feeling, and a sinking sensation in her belly, which told her she was a stone-cold liar.

CHAPTER SEVENTEEN

St. Eustace was a small island. The kind that it doesn't take more than four or five hours to circumnavigate, depending on the time of day, and how fast you drive. But to Kiah it suddenly appeared to have grown to the width of Canada, since it seemed to take forever to get back to Port Michael.

Mina had called a couple of times, updating them, and Kiah had almost lost his mind when she told him that Neil Jonas had performed a lumbar puncture on Charm.

He hadn't said anything untoward, he didn't think, but even with the knowledge that it had been successfully done, and Charm had been admitted pending the results, he was enraged.

"Hezekiah, you know Mina would never agree to anything she didn't think was necessary," Granny said, but her voice wobbled, showing how badly all of this was affecting her, too.

"They shouldn't have done it without my permission. They could have called—"

"You told them Mina would make the decisions until you got there, and she did as you asked. Do you think it would have been an easy one to make? Would it have been easy for you?"

But Kiah was in a head space where logic couldn't touch him, where rage sustained his sanity, keeping all other emotions and impulses at bay.

When they finally arrived at the hospital in Port Michael, he was a ball of fury, ready to let fly at anyone who got in his way.

Neil Jonas was at the nurses' station when he got up to the wards, and Kiah found himself wanting to punch him in the face. When the other man saw him approaching and gave him a solemn nod, the urge only increased.

"It's definitely viral encephalitis," Neil said after a brief greeting. "The lab results just came back, and I've ordered treatment. I want to keep her in for a couple of days under observation, but although it's a bad case, it was caught early enough, and she'll make a full recovery."

"Thank the Father," was Miss Pearl's response, but although the news was good, it did nothing to lessen the churning ball of anger in Kiah's belly.

When he entered the hospital room and found Mina sitting beside Charm's bed, not even the sight of her worn, tired face could touch him.

Only Charm's wan smile somehow cut

through his rage, and he moved to her side, leaning down to kiss her forehead.

"How are you feeling, sweetheart?"

"A bit better," she said. "They said the headache should go away soon, but Auntie's made them turn the lights down for me. And I have to lie still, because of the thing they did to my back." She looked past him to say, "Hello, Granny."

"Why you want to scare an old lady like me, Charmaine?" Miss Pearl took one of Charm's hands and bent down for a kiss. "My heart can't take the stress."

"I didn't mean to, Granny. You know I didn't." Charm sounded genuinely contrite, and Miss Pearl chuckled in response.

"I do know you didn't mean to. I'm just teasing you."

"Sit here, Miss Pearl," Mina said, having already got up from the lone chair in the room. "I'll see if I can find another chair from somewhere."

Kiah hadn't looked at her, after that first glance, but now he knew he needed to vent some of the ire still filling his chest, and the one who seemed to deserve it most had just walked away.

"I'll be right back, Charm," he said. "Granny, stay with her for me, please?"

"Uncle, wait." Charm caught hold of his hand,

making Kiah pause. "Can you bring me something to eat? I'm hungry."

"Okay, love." He bent to kiss her forehead again, and then strode out of the room, looking for Mina.

When there was no sight of her, he went over to the nurses' desk.

"Did you see which way Dr. Haraldson went?"

The nurse on duty pointed toward the door leading to the stairs, and Kiah made a beeline for it.

When he opened the door, he didn't hear footsteps, but there was a soft, almost imperceptible sound echoing in the stairwell. It seemed to be coming from above him and so, although the rising staircase led only to the roof access, which was always locked, he went up, instead of down. Turning the corner on the landing, he could see her, sitting on the top step, her hand to her face, rocking back and forth.

She must have heard his footsteps, because she looked up, but her tear-stained face and reddened eyes couldn't melt the icy fury in his heart.

It must have shown in his eyes, or expression, because she got up, the tears still rolling down her cheeks.

"Kiah, please don't be angry with me right now. I don't think I could stand it."

She sounded so defeated, so sad, and it was then he realized: he wasn't angry with her.

All the fury inside was aimed squarely at himself.

He was the one who'd put her in a position to make the heart-wrenching decision about the lumbar puncture, who'd caused her the pain so clearly etched on her face.

"I did what I thought was right, for Charm." The words came out in little bursts, in between her sobs. "You know I'd never do anything to hurt her, if I could h-help it."

He wanted to tell her he knew, and understood, but all the old terror and agony he'd carried through the years clogged his throat.

All the fear came back, beating at him, as though to break him. Swamping him, until he thought he might drown.

Suddenly he was twelve again, watching his father die, impotent to help. Having his mother blame him, although he'd done the only thing he'd known how, which was call for an ambulance. And then he was thirty, getting the call about Karlene and Roy, learning he'd failed to give them the help and support they'd needed to get through the toughest of times.

And now, he'd put the responsibility of Charm's care on Mina's shoulders, instead of taking it on his own, the way he should. Making Mina cry, in a way he'd only seen her break down once before, at the loss of her hand.

Then, to make it worse, he'd gotten angry, when it was all his fault.

How could he do that? Cause so much pain, and translate that into the kind of rage that made him want to punch the walls, shout at the top of his lungs? It was all he could do to close his eyes, stand motionless, lock his knees, so as not to kick and scream.

"Kiah—"

Mina's voice broke through the bombardment of his thoughts, and he realized she was holding him, her arm around his waist, her hand cupping his cheek, her worried gaze searching his.

She was holding *him*, as if he was the one in need of sympathy, of reassurance.

Once more he'd failed at doing the right thing.

Unable to speak, to articulate everything swirling and snapping in his chest, he bent and kissed Mina's forehead, his heart breaking all over again, as tears filled her eyes once more.

"Kiah, she's going to be okay. That's what's important."

But he couldn't hear that right now, not with any kind of equanimity. All he could do was ease out of Mina's embrace and walk away, hoping to get some kind of control over himself, before he did any more harm.

* * *

Mina made it as far as the ladies' room before she lost it again, hiding in a stall to shed some more tears, although they made her feel worse than before.

Damn Kiah. Damn him straight to hell and back, for making her feel as though she hadn't done her best. As though she had somehow failed him and Charm.

She couldn't find it in her heart to forgive him. Not yet. Maybe never.

All the years of friendship and understanding, the connection they'd shared, had been shattered, because he apparently didn't trust her to do right by a little girl she loved, probably almost as much as he did.

How else could she interpret his actions, the anger she'd seen in his expression?

While staying with Charm as she had the lumbar puncture, hearing her cry and trying to soothe her, she'd hardly been able to stand it. The love she had for Charm was so strong it almost rivaled that which she had for Kiah himself.

Had he forgotten all she'd been through with his niece, or not understood how special it was to her? Not recognized Mina would never, ever do anything to harm the little girl?

She'd thought she'd been hurt before, but somehow this was bigger, more painful than even the loss of her hand. And she wasn't sure how she was going to face Kiah, after how he'd made her feel.

How could he have placed so much trust in her in the past, and lost confidence in her when it was a matter of life and death? Charm's life or death?

His lack of faith gutted her, made her feel hollow and bereft. Without his trust, could they even maintain the friendship they had?

And now she realized making love with him had been an even bigger mistake than she'd suspected. It had tied her to him in ways she could never truly undo.

Well, the joke was on her, wasn't it? She'd made the mistake of falling for her best friend, only to realize the relationship, even the friendship, wasn't what she'd thought. She'd always love him, but had to accept they were at the end of the road.

Grabbing some more tissue from the dispenser, she mopped at her eyes and blew her nose.

She'd put off making a decision about her future for too long, and now she had a clear direction.

There was no way she'd stay on St. Eustace and potentially see Kiah every day. If she were being brutally honest with herself, she'd been leaning heavily toward staying. She loved it here, loved being around Charm and Miss Pearl, and felt she could do a lot of good, professionally, on the island. Real work that would make an impact on those around her, and maybe even for years to come. The thought of going back to the rush and scurry of Canada hadn't held much appeal, even with the prestigious job on offer.

She was a different woman from the one who'd have jumped, just over a year ago, at the deputy chief position and worked herself into the ground to be successful at it. Now, if she did decide to take it, she had to be assured she could still maintain a healthy balance between the job and the life she knew she wanted.

There was a high probability she wouldn't even take the job at all. After all, no one needed to know whether she was going to, or not. She just had to turn down the job here, and tell them she was going back, once she'd fulfilled her obligations to the hospital.

How was she going to manage for the rest of the time she was on the island, without doing or saying something to Kiah they'd both regret? As angry as she was with him, she knew she'd get past it, but nothing would ever be the same. She'd have to hide behind a mask of friendly laughter, so as not to upset Charm, or get Miss Pearl on her case.

It all felt untenable, made her want to run away. Just curl up somewhere alone, like she'd done after the divorce and the loss of her hand.

But that wasn't an option.

She was committed to staying on St. Eustace, at least for a little longer, and not even Kiah's foolishness was going to stop her from doing what she'd promised.

If there was one good thing about the situation, she thought, as she made her way out of the stall and over to the sink to wash her face, it was that it no doubt put paid to the physical relationship with Kiah.

She couldn't share her body with a man who couldn't trust her when the chips were down. Couldn't trust her to be a good custodian of his niece's life.

No matter what arguments her wayward libido and her breaking heart might come up with.

Bracing herself to see him again, Mina went back to Charm's room. Kiah wasn't there and Charm was asleep under Miss Pearl's watchful eyes.

The older lady got up as soon as Mina came in, and pulled her in for a hug. How was it that Miss Pearl suddenly felt frailer than she had before, as though the fright of Charm's illness had sapped the strength from her body?

"Mina, child, thank you for being there for

Charm," she whispered. "And for acting so promptly. I'm so glad you were with her, although I know it must have been hard."

Mina hugged her back, thankful that at least someone appreciated what she'd done, and been through.

"It wasn't easy, but she's going to be all right, and that's the important thing."

Miss Pearl leaned back and cupped Mina's cheeks, her gaze searching.

"It is, child. It is. But you must be exhausted from all this drama and excitement. Hezekiah hasn't come back yet, and I'm going to stay with her for a while. Why don't you go and get some rest? You can come back later and sit with her, if you want."

Glad for the excuse to go, Mina nodded.

"Call me and let me know what time my shift is, and I'll come back. I'll take a cab and leave the car here, so Kiah has it to use."

"You drove yourself and Charm here?" The expression of shock on Miss Pearl's face would normally be comical, but Mina had no energy left for laughter.

"Yes. I didn't want to wait for a cab or an ambulance," she said, fishing the keys out of her bag and putting them on the table.

"Well," said Miss Pearl quietly, as Mina bent to kiss her cheek, prepared to take her leave.

"What doesn't happen in a year happens in a day. You're well on your way to full recovery, and it makes my old heart glad to see it."

As Mina walked toward the door, Miss Pearl said, "Mina, do me a favor before you go?"

Mina paused, almost too weary to turn back, but doing it anyway. "Of course."

The elderly lady hesitated for an instant, and then said, slowly, "Hezekiah said he was going to get Charmaine something to eat, but I'm worried about him. Could you check on him, please?"

Tears threatened, but Mina held them back. "I saw him. I think he's okay. Just angry, I guess because of the lumbar puncture."

Miss Pearl shook her head. "No, child. That's not why he's angry." She sighed, lowering herself back into the chair. "Ever since his father died, he's taken the weight of this family onto his shoulders. That mother of his blamed him for not saving Benjamin—his father—and for everything else she could come up with. Kiah's probably blaming himself for not being here with Charm, and for putting the burden of her care onto you."

Legs suddenly weak, Mina reached out and held on to the doorjamb to hold herself up. "His mother did that? He never told me."

Miss Pearl nodded, her eyes solemn behind her glasses. "I thank God every day that Kiah turned out as well as he did, but he takes on more responsibility than he should, because of that woman and her bad ways. And when things frighten or hurt him, he gets angry, like a lot of men do. It's the only way he knows how to let it out."

And Mina knew how his mother's anger had scarred Kiah, both physically and emotionally. He'd said, more than once, when they were teens, how much he feared turning out like her, bitter and abusive.

Did he still feel that way? Get frightened by his reactions, instead of realizing they were natural and not dangerous?

Had he walked away not because he was angry with Mina, but because he fighting his inner demons, and was afraid he'd take them out on her?

There was only one way to find out.

She straightened, determination giving her back her strength.

"I'll find him, Miss Pearl, and make sure he's all right."

CHAPTER EIGHTEEN

SHE SEARCHED THE hospital for Kiah, finally finding him pacing back and forth in the sanctuary garden behind the chapel. The sun was setting, roseate color tinting the sky and the water in the little fountain, but Kiah was clearly oblivious to it all. Head down, he walked back and forth, his hands clenched into fists, each stride taken as though he was trying to push his feet through the earth's crust.

With her new perspective, just watching him made her heart hurt. His pain was obvious in each step he took, the pallor of his face unmistakable.

Not wanting to startle him, but knowing he hadn't noticed her, Mina stepped onto the stone path and walked toward him. His head came up at the sound of her first footfall, and there, in his eyes, she saw his agony before he had a chance to mask it.

"Do you remember the professor at university who told us to make sure we took up a hobby?" she asked.

Kiah gave her a blank look, and then, blinking

as though just awaking up, he nodded. "Professor Brathwaite, wasn't it?"

Mina snapped her fingers. "Yes, that's the one. Anatomy."

His brows came together. "What made you think of him?"

She shrugged, stopping at the neat little stacked-stone wall surrounding the garden and sitting on it. "I guess it was watching you marching back and forth like that. If pacing were a sport, you'd be a shoo-in for an Olympic medal."

The sound he made wasn't quite a laugh, but it was close. Then he immediately sobered. "Is Charm—?"

"She's fine. Sleeping, with Miss Pearl standing guard over her. We were worried about you. I wanted to check on you before I left."

"I'm fine." It came out a little like a growl, but then he repeated it, in a softer tone. "I'm fine. I just need some time to…"

"Decompress?"

"As good a word as any. Mina, I can't—"

She held up her hand, forestalling his words. "You can, Kiah. You can tell me what's going on in that head of yours."

His lips twisted, and he shook his head. "No, I can't. Not right now."

"Why?"

Kiah turned away, fists clenched again, and

she saw the tension in the stiffness of his back, the taut line of his neck.

"Leave it, Mina. We can talk about it later."

"I think we should deal with it now."

He didn't reply, just took a couple steps away from her, as though distancing himself from the conversation.

From her.

Trying not to be hurt by that, she didn't move, although it was clear he wished she would just go away. It was up to her to get him to open up, and she wasn't sure how.

So she said the first thing that came to mind. "I was scared, when I realized how ill Charm was, and angry. Even now, I'm still pretty angry."

He froze, his shoulders bowing, and Mina rushed into speech, before he could start taking the blame for that, too.

"I'm angry because she's ill, because no child should have to go through what she's gone through. But the one thing I'm not is angry at you. Are you angry at me?"

That brought him around to face her, and his expression was so anguished she could hardly bear it.

"No! God, Mina, I never wanted you to think that."

"Then what *are* you angry about, Kiah?"

He spun away and then back, as though he couldn't help himself.

"Everything," he said, his voice gravelly, as though he held the volume down by sheer will. "That Charm was ill, and I wasn't here to help her. That you had to be the one to make that call, and stay with her during the spinal tap. That—"

He stopped. Cursing, he turned away once more.

She got up, needing to be on her feet, caught somewhere between anger and pain—both for him. All for him.

"Don't turn away from me, Kiah. Face me and tell me the rest of it."

"Stop it, Mina."

It was a plea, but one she had to ignore. For him and, she suspected, for her, too.

"Stop what? Stop trying to be your friend, or trying to help you? Is that what you want, Kiah?"

"No." He still had his back to her and threw the word over his shoulder, as though he couldn't stop it from emerging from his throat. "I never wanted to hurt you, Mina, and yet I did, by asking you to take up a responsibility that was mine."

Moving a little closer, she said, "You didn't hurt me, Kiah, by asking that of me. I love Charm, and I was honored you'd put her care in my hands."

"But I shouldn't have."

"Why not?"

"It wasn't your burden to bear!" He almost shouted it, making Mina jump, startled. "It was mine, and I sloughed it off onto you and made you deal with it, hurting you in the process."

He stopped, and she could see his chest heaving, as though he'd run a mile, rather than been standing still.

"Is that it?" she said, infusing as much annoyance into her voice as she could, when all she wanted to do was go and hold him. "I'm this fragile little flower you have to protect from the vagaries of life?"

"You know I didn't mean it that way…"

"Really? Because that's how it sounded."

That made him face her, and she saw the anger still shimmering behind his eyes.

"I am trying to protect you. Can't you see that? I'm angry, Mina. Furious. And I just need a little time to get myself back together so I don't explode. Can you give that to me?"

"No…" She shook her head, seeing his eyes widen, as though that were the last thing he expected. "I'm your friend, and I'm here to listen to you rage, to scream with you, if that's what you want. To hug you, if you need me to. Keeping it all in won't help, Kiah. It'll only hurt."

The look he gave her was incendiary, and made the hair on the back of her neck stand up. But there was no way she was backing down.

"I don't want you to do any of those things." It sounded as though his throat was tight, the words harsh. "I can manage this on my own."

She nodded slowly, holding back the pain of his rejection, not letting it weaken her resolve.

"So as not to take it out on anyone else?"

"Yes! Dammit Mina, just leave me to it, won't you?"

Instead of walking away, she stepped closer to him, saw the way he stiffened.

"You know you're not your mother, don't you?"

He stepped back, his head tilting away, as though she'd slapped him.

"What did you say?"

It was barely above a whisper, but he might as well have shouted it, for the emotional punch it packed.

"You're not your mother, Kiah. You don't hurt people because you're angry. You don't throw things, threaten people, lose your cool and intentionally say hurtful things. You have a temper, but you control it and, at times like this, you need to let the anger out with someone who cares, who understands and isn't afraid to stand with you while you do."

He stepped back again, the movement jerky, instinctive. She followed, keeping pace with him.

"You don't know what you're saying."

"Really?" Mina stepped even closer, so they were only a couple feet apart. "I was there, at school, when you came in with that cut on your head. You told everyone you'd fallen, but I got you to admit your mother threw a bottle at you. I asked you what you did, when that happened, and you said you locked yourself in the bathroom. You didn't hurt her back, although you could have, easily."

"Mina…don't."

Again she ignored his pleading tone, knowing it all needed to be said.

"And when you were on the football field, senior year, and the opposing player was calling you nasty names, trying to get you to fight, I saw how angry you were, but you wouldn't give in to it."

"I destroyed a garbage can." He said it as though making an important point, but she waved it off.

"After the game, outside, when it was just the two of us around. Did you hurt anyone? No, you didn't. And there was the time in university, when those two guys jumped you. You fought back, but once they were down, you walked away. You could have kicked the hell out of them, but you didn't."

"Stop."

He sounded so tired suddenly, beaten, but she wasn't sure she'd gotten through to him yet.

"I'll stop when I think you understand what I'm saying. The people who love you know the man you are. We're not afraid of your temper, and while we love how protective you are, we don't need you to feel as though you're responsible for our lives, because you're not."

She moved closer, so as to put her hand on his arm, and his muscles, already tight, hardened even further under her fingers.

"And sometimes you have to accept that someone other than you is going to do the protecting. I was glad I was the one who made the decision about Charm today, so that you didn't have to. I knew how much it would hurt you to have to agree to the lumbar puncture, how it would tear you up to see her go through it, so I did that for you, out of love."

"I don't like to see you hurting."

"I know," she said softly, raising her hand to place it against his cheek, meeting his still-anguished gaze. "But sometimes it's inevitable, and you know that, as a human, a doctor, a man. You just have to accept it."

Turning his head to kiss her palm, he closed his eyes, and her heart ached to see him so vulnerable.

He took a deep, shuddering breath. "What am I going to do without you, when you're gone?"

Everything she felt for him swelled inside her, and she knew she had to find the courage to speak her truth, no matter the consequences.

"You don't have to find out, if you don't want to."

In a blink she found her gaze captured by his, and the tenderness of the previous moments fled before the intensity in his eyes.

But he didn't speak, didn't ask what she meant, just froze, almost as though he'd even stopped breathing.

"I love you, Kiah, more than I ever thought I could love anyone, and I want to stay here with you. But you have to decide whether you want me to, or not."

She almost stopped, too afraid to continue, but she was stronger now than she had been, and she needed him to know she accepted and loved him, just the way he was. So she inhaled and found the courage, even though her hand was shaking and her knees were watery.

"It scares me, Kiah, loving you this way.

You'll never lose my friendship, but we could be so much more, and I can get past the fear because I know our lives would be better, together. I want you for my own, to help you raise Charm, even if we never have any children of our own, since that's not something you want. Be there for you through good times and bad, just like we've always been there for each other since that first day in Mrs. Nowac's class. All I want, all I need, is you."

He still hadn't moved, or spoken, so Mina rubbed his cheek lightly, savoring the warmth of his skin on her palm, then she pulled away.

"Or I can go back to Toronto, and we salvage what we can, from a distance."

It was up to him now, but she thought her heart would break when she turned to leave, and he didn't call her back.

Kiah tried to take in all the things Mina had said, as he watched her walk away, but her words swirled in his head, until he could hardly make sense of them anymore. His heart pounded, and his chest felt tight, so he could only draw shallow draughts of air into his lungs.

This was what love did to a man. Tied him in knots, scrambled his brains, left him without the wherewithal to know his head from his butt.

She'd always had this effect on him. Even

when they were bantering back and forth, he'd been awestruck that Mina was his friend, that she actually liked him enough to stick around.

And from the first day they'd met, he would have done anything for her, up to and including laying down his own life.

She'd said she loved him, wanted to be with him, and then, in almost the same breath, said she was willing to leave and go back to Toronto.

The memory of her saying it slashed through the fog filling his head, even as his stomach twisted with emotions too numerous to categorize.

She'd said she was willing to give up on her dream of having a family of her own, just to be with him, but did she really mean it? He'd heard what she said—about his temper, about him not being like his mother—but did he believe it?

He wasn't sure he was willing to take the chance to find out. It terrified him to imagine himself turning into the monster he knew he was capable of becoming.

Yet, as he'd told Charm, Mina never said anything she didn't mean. She knew him, better than sometimes he knew himself. Was it possible to believe in himself the way she did?

Moreover, could he stand to lose her?

Let her go back to Toronto, taking the light

and love and happiness she'd given him back with her?

Now he felt almost physically ill, and had to swallow against the burning lump that formed in his throat, and that sensation swamped all other emotions.

She was right, as she usually was. He'd let his fears rule his life, clung to the painful past instead of letting it go and living. But the fear of losing her was greater than any other, and he knew he couldn't do it.

And something else she'd said was true, too: they were better, together. Always had been, since he was twelve years old, and had first looked into those sparkling brown eyes.

She'd been there for him during the best and worst times of his life, steadfast and strong, cheering him on, lifting him up.

Mina was everything to him. She brought peace and joy into his heart, and comfort to his ragged and battered soul. He loved her more than he thought he could ever love.

Thank goodness he'd finally found the sense, and the courage, to admit it.

And he'd let her walk away thinking he didn't care enough to try to stop her.

Cursing himself for a fool, he took off after her, and finally caught up just as she was about to get into Mr. Brown's taxi, in front of the hospital's main doors.

There was so much he wanted to say, to tell her, but all he could do at that moment was call her name.

Mina turned, her eyes widening as she realized what he was about to do.

But she didn't resist when he pulled her into his arms and kissed her, as though he never planned to stop.

"Woo-ee! Wait 'til Miss Pearl hear 'bout this!"

It was the sound of Mr. Brown's hooting that finally had them breaking the kiss, but Kiah didn't let her go. Instead, he spent a moment just staring into her eyes, soaking up the love shining there.

Then he bent his head to whisper into her ear. "Now we're going to have to listen to Granny crow. She's been angling for us to get together for years."

She giggled, burying her face in his shoulder as Mr. Brown continued to tell everyone who passed by how Dr. K "grab up Dr. Mina and kiss her."

"Tell me you love me again, Mina."

He needed to hear it, even though she was trembling in his arms and holding him so tight he knew it would be forever.

"I love you, Kiah. And I always will."

"Ah, sweet girl, I love you, too."

"You all goin' have to get married, you know." When they both looked around, Mr. Brown was frowning, and had his hands on his hips. The stance and expression made him look remarkably like Granny, despite his being at least twenty years her junior. "Or Miss Pearl goin' beat you."

Kiah looked down into Mina's shining face and couldn't help grinning.

"What you say, sweet girl? We have to keep Granny happy."

She gave him a scowl, which was belied by the gleam in her eyes. "Hezekiah Langdon, if you think I'm taking that secondhand proposal, you clearly don't know me as well as you should, after all these years. Do it right, and I might say yes."

"Might? Just might?"

"If you're lucky, or unlucky, depending on how you want to look at it."

"Oh, I'm the luckiest man in the world, having you in my life and in my arms, and I know it."

Then, to the amusement and delight of everyone standing around and gawking, he sealed that statement with another long kiss.

"And as for girl, I love you too."

"You all goin' have to get married. You know," when they both looked around, Mr. Brown was frowning, still with his hands on his hips. The stance and expression made him look re—

EPILOGUE

MINA PUT HER hand on Kiah's arm, squeezing it with perhaps a little more force than was really necessary.

At least in his opinion.

"Stop glaring at that boy, Hezekiah. You're going to make him pee his pants."

She'd whispered it out of the corner of her mouth, obviously trying to be discreet. Kiah had no such reservations.

"Good. At least then I'll know *he* knows who's the boss."

"Come back inside and give them some privacy," she said, tugging him away from the back door and the veranda, where Charm and Ramesh were sitting.

"They don't need privacy. They're too young for privacy," he grumbled, even as he was letting her lead him through into the living room. "I don't know why they couldn't sit in here with us."

Mina just chuckled, and Granny gave him one of her dry looks.

"Charm is sixteen now, Kiah. You have to

give her some leeway. After all, you were the one who said she could start dating at this age."

"Me? Oh, hell no. I think my plan was that she didn't start until she was thirty. Mina begged for her, and now this is what we've got. Ramesh on the back veranda."

"But you've known Ramesh for years." Mina sank onto the couch with a heartfelt sigh, and patted the cushion beside her, until he sat down too. "And you like him."

"I *liked* Ramesh, until he started giving Charm those longing looks. Now I'm not too sure."

Mina giggled, then groaned. "Stop being such a fuddy-duddy and rub my feet for me. That operation yesterday has me aching all over."

Given a new topic to worry over, Kiah sank his teeth into it, even as he reached out and gently received the body parts that needed attention onto his lap.

"As for that, why did you think it a good idea, at seven months pregnant, to supervise a five-hour operation? Couldn't John have done that? You've been training him to take over while you're on maternity leave."

"He's good, but I need to make sure we can deliver what we say we can." She gave a little moan of appreciation when Kiah rubbed her arches. "John will do fine, and I've promised to be on call, just in case, but that hip surgery was complex, and I wanted to supervise it myself."

"Well, no more of that. You need to take better care of yourself, and our daughter."

Mina chuckled. "Aye, aye, Captain," she replied with a saucy expression on her beloved face.

Just looking at her made him content, filled his heart with joy and the kind of peace that had eluded him most of his life. This second pregnancy was unplanned, but Kiah had been elated when it happened. It wasn't ideal for Mina's health that their son, asleep in his crib, would only be seventeen months older than his sister, but Mina's prenatal checkups had been good, and he loved how happy she was.

He hadn't thought it possible, but he loved her a little more every day. Thank God he hadn't let his fears drive her away. She'd given him time and space to consider the question of children, not saying anything about it until he'd brought it up himself. This second pregnancy was, though, the last, according to Mina.

"Three is enough," she'd said, once she'd gotten over the shock, and he'd agreed, although, secretly, he wouldn't mind one more. Since he wasn't the one bearing or having to deliver the child, whether to have another or not wasn't a choice he felt qualified to make.

He heard Charm's laughter faintly, since he'd left the door open, and his attention was snagged once more.

"I wonder what's going on out there," he grumbled, wishing he could see through the walls separating them. "I'm thinking of putting cameras up around the house. For security reasons," he added quickly, when Miss Pearl gave him a withering look.

Mina started laughing so hard she held her belly, as though it hurt.

"What's so funny?" he asked, pinching her little toe.

"I was just thinking," she said, hardly able to get the words out through her continued mirth. "By the time you get over Charm growing up and dating, it will be time for this little one to start."

"Oh, mercy," he groaned, horrified by the thought. "Are you trying to make me go gray, all at once? Don't say things like that."

"And if she follows family tradition, we better start looking at any boy she meets when she's twelve, just in case."

"Yes," he agreed, chuckling with her, caught up in her amusement. "Apparently we fall in love young, and never get over it."

"Who better to fall for but your best friend?"

she asked, sending him a look so full of love his heart stuttered with pleasure.

"No one, my sweet girl. No one."

* * * * *

If you enjoyed this story, check out
these other great reads from
Ann McIntosh

Awakened by Her Brooding Brazilian
The Nurse's Christmas Temptation
Surgeon Prince, Cinderella Bride
The Surgeon's One Night to Forever

All available now!